'We... ...g... ...
for a relationship, Anna. You've
...and
now you will have to accept the
consequences.'

'What consequences?' The colour seemed to
drain out of her face.

'What do you think?' Dante snarled, his hands
curling into fists down by his sides. 'What
do you *think* will happen now that I know I
fathered a child that night? Did you think I
would calmly walk away, saying *Oh, well*?
From this moment on I fully intend to be a
father to our daughter—and that means I want
a legalised relationship with her mother…'

The day **Maggie Cox** saw the film version of *Wuthering Heights*, with a beautiful Merle Oberon and a very handsome Laurence Olivier, was the day she became hooked on romance. From that day onwards she spent a lot of time dreaming up her own romances, secretly hoping that one day she might become published and get paid for doing what she loved most! Now that her dream is being realised, she wakes up every morning and counts her blessings. She is married to a gorgeous man, and is the mother of two wonderful sons. Her two other great passions in life—besides her family and reading/writing—are music and films.

MISTRESS, MOTHER...WIFE?

BY
MAGGIE COX

MILLS & BOON

All the characters in this book have no existence outside the imagination of the author, and have no relation whatsoever to anyone bearing the same name or names. They are not even distantly inspired by any individual known or unknown to the author, and all the incidents are pure invention.

All Rights Reserved including the right of reproduction in whole or in part in any form. This edition is published by arrangement with Harlequin Enterprises II B.V./S.à.r.l. The text of this publication or any part thereof may not be reproduced or transmitted in any form or by any means, electronic or mechanical, including photocopying, recording, storage in an information retrieval system, or otherwise, without the written permission of the publisher.

This book is sold subject to the condition that it shall not, by way of trade or otherwise, be lent, resold, hired out or otherwise circulated without the prior consent of the publisher in any form of binding or cover other than that in which it is published and without a similar condition including this condition being imposed on the subsequent purchaser.

® and TM are trademarks owned and used by the trademark owner and/or its licensee. Trademarks marked with ® are registered with the United Kingdom Patent Office and/or the Office for Harmonisation in the Internal Market and in other countries.

First published in Great Britain 2011
Harlequin Mills & Boon Limited,
Eton House, 18-24 Paradise Road, Richmond, Surrey TW9 1SR

© Maggie Cox 2011

ISBN: 978 0 263 88627 6

Harlequin Mills & Boon policy is to use papers that are natural, renewable and recyclable products and made from wood grown in sustainable forests. The logging and manufacturing process conform to the legal environmental regulations of the country of origin.

Printed and bound in Spain
by Litografia Rosés, S.A., Barcelona

MISTRESS, MOTHER…WIFE?

To my singing teacher, Jeanette Barnes,
who has become a good friend and
makes the most comforting cup of tea in the world!

CHAPTER ONE

IT WAS a pastime she liked to employ when things got a little slower towards the end of the evening. She'd scan the remaining customers who were lingering over their drinks at tables or at the bar and conjure up a tale about them. Making up stories was meat and drink to Anna… it was the thing that had kept her sane and protected when she was a child. Her little made-up worlds had all been so much safer and fulfilling than reality, and there were many, many times she'd sought refuge there.

Now, as though tugged by a powerful magnet, yet again she considered the handsome, square-jawed individual staring into space in the furthermost corner of the room. He'd occupied the stylish burgundy armchair for at least two hours now, had neither removed his coat nor glanced interestedly at the other well-heeled patrons even once. It was as though they were completely off his radar. All he seemed to be focused on was the inner screen of his own troubled mind.

There was definitely an intense, preoccupied air about him that intrigued Anna. After all, what dreamer with a yen for making up stories *wouldn't* be intrigued or provoked by such fascinating material? Making sure she was discreet, she studied him hard. She hadn't personally looked into his eyes yet, but already she guessed they would have the power to hynotise whoever was caught in their gaze. A small shiver ran down her spine.

Having checked the room to see if she was needed anywhere, she let her gaze return to the mystery man. He had straight mid-blond hair, with hints of silver in it, and appeared to be growing out a cut that had probably been both stylish and expensive. Everything about him exuded wealth and good taste, a well as the sense of power and entitlement that often accompanied those attributes. Although his eye-catching broad shoulders appeared weighed down by his concerns, he also wore a fierce need for privacy that was like an invisible electronic gate, warning all comers that they encroached upon his space at their peril. Had an important deal gone sour? Had someone deceived him or seriously let him down in some way? *He didn't look like a man who suffered fools gladly.*

Anna sighed, then studied him again. No...she'd got it all wrong. The black coat he was wearing suddenly sang out to her. He'd lost someone close. Yes, that was it. He was grieving. That was why his expression was so haunted and morose. As she studied his formidable chiselled profile, with the deep shadow of a cleft centred in that square-cut chin, it seemed almost impertinent to speculate about him further if she'd guessed the truth. *Poor man...* He must be feeling totally wretched.

The third Scotch on the rocks he'd ordered was drained right down to the bottom of the glass, Anna noticed. Would he be ordering another one? Bitter personal experience had taught her that alcohol never solved anything. *All it had done for her father was make his black moods even blacker.*

The hotel bar closed at eleven-thirty and it was already a quarter past, she saw. Collecting a tray, she circumnavigated the tables with her usual light step, her heart thudding like a brick dropped into a millpond as she overrode her natural inclination to stay well clear. In front of the man, she schooled her lips into a pleasant smile.

'I'm sorry to disturb you, sir, but will you be requiring another drink? Only, the bar will be closing soon.'

Glittering blue-grey eyes that contained all the warmth of a perilous icy sea swivelled to survey her. For a startled second Anna told herself it served her right if she received a frosty reception, when his body language clearly signalled that he wanted to be left alone. But just then a corner of the austere masculine mouth lifted in the mocking semblance of a smile.

'What do you think? Do I look like I'm in need of another drink, beautiful?'

There was the faintest Mediterranean edge to his otherwise British accent. But in any case he was wrong. *She wasn't beautiful.* If it weren't for the rippling waist-length auburn hair that she freed from her workday style every night when her shift ended, Anna would consider herself quite ordinary. Yet the unexpected compliment—mocking or otherwise—was as though he'd lit a brightly burning candle inside her.

'I wouldn't presume to think I knew what you needed, sir.'

'Call me Dan,' he said, giving her the commonly abbreviated form of his name which he went by in London, not wanting to hear Dante, the name his mother had gifted him with, tonight of all nights.

The invitation almost caused her to stumble. She dipped her head beneath the glare of his riveting gaze because it was almost too powerful to look into for long.

'We're not supposed to address the customers personally,' she answered.

'And do you always follow the rules to the letter?'

'I do if I want to keep my job.'

'This establishment would be extremely foolish if they were to get rid of a girl like you.'

'You don't even know me.'

'Maybe I'd like to.' His smile was slow and deliberate. 'Get to know you better, I mean.'

That roguish grin was like a guided missile that hit all her sensitive spots at once. Inside, the implosion almost rocked Anna off her feet.

'I don't think you do,' she remarked, serious-voiced.

'You're probably just looking for a handy diversion, if the truth be known.'

'Really? A diversion from what, exactly?' A dark blond eyebrow with tiny glints of copper in it lifted in amusement.

'From whatever unhappy thoughts that have been bothering you.'

The smile vanished. His expression became as guarded as though a wall made of three-foot-deep granite had thundered down in front of it.

'How do you know I'm disturbed by unhappy thoughts? What are you…a mind-reader?'

'No.' Anna's teeth nibbled anxiously at her lip. 'I just observe people and—and sense things about them.'

'What a dangerous occupation. And you're compelled to do this why? You don't have any of your own material to contemplate? You must be a rare human being indeed if that's the case…to have managed to negotiate your way through life without any problems at all.'

'I haven't…gone through life without any problems, I mean. How would I have learned anything or be able to empathise with other people if I'd been problem-free? I'd also be quite superficial…which I'm not.'

'And here I was, thinking you were just a simple, uncomplicated barmaid, when in fact you're clearly quite the little philosopher.'

Anna didn't take the comment as an insult. How could she? As well as the pain glittering in his winter-coloured eyes, locked inside his scathing tone was the suggestion of the blackest kind of despair.

A heartfelt desire to help ease it in some way swept passionately through her.

'I'm not looking for trouble… You just seemed so alone and sad, sitting there, that I thought that if you wanted to talk…well, I'd be a good listener. Sometimes it's easier to tell your troubles to a stranger than someone you know. But anyway, if you think that's impertinent of me, and another drink would help more, then I'll gladly get you one.'

The man who'd told her to call him Dan raised a shoulder, then dropped it again dismissively.

'I'm not the unburdening kind, and if you were hoping I might be then I have to tell you that you're wasting your time. What's your name?'

'Anna.'

'That's it…just Anna?'

'Anna Bailey.'

A cold sweat broke out across her skin, where previously his disturbing glance had kindled the kind of heat that made dry tinder burst into flames. Was he going to report her or something? She hadn't meant to insult him. Her only desire had been to help if she could. Was he an important enough customer for a complaint from him to help her lose her job? *She prayed not.*

The comfortable family-run hotel in a quiet corner of Covent Garden had become her home for the past three years, and she loved everything about it—including her work. She didn't even mind if she sometimes had to work long hours. Her employers were so kind—generous to a fault, in fact—and her recent pay-rise had helped make life a whole lot more comfortable than when she'd worked at jobs she'd hated and for too little money. Lord knew she didn't want to go back to struggling again.

'Look, Mr, er...'

'I told you to call me Dan.'

'I can't do that.'

'Why?' he snapped, his expression irritated.

'Because it wouldn't be professional. I'm an employee here and you're a guest.'

'Yet you offered me a shoulder to cry on. Is that on offer to all your guests, Anna?'

She flushed. 'Of course not. I just wanted to—'

'So the only thing that prevents you calling me by my first name is that you're a stickler for the rules and you work here, while I'm a paying customer?'

'I'd better go.'

'No—stay. Is there any other reason you can't be more informal? Like the fact that you've got a husband or boyfriend waiting for you at home, perhaps?'

Anna stared helplessly.

'No.' She cleared her throat, then glanced round to see if anyone was observing them.

Brian—her young, dark-haired colleague—was wiping down the half-moon-shaped bar and chatting to a customer at the same time, whilst a smartly dressed middle-aged couple sat tenderly holding hands as they lingered over their after-theatre drinks. They'd regaled Anna earlier with tales of the play they'd been to, and their infectious enjoyment was contagious. Twenty-five years married and they were still like young lovers around each other.

Sighing, she turned back to find him broodingly examining her. The sudden jolt of her heartbeat mimicked another heavy brick splashing into a pond as his glance interestedly and deliberately appraised her figure. His gaze lingered boldly on the curve of her hips and the swell of her breasts, trailing sensuous fire in its wake. There was nothing provocative about the purple silk blouse with its pretty Chinese collar and the straight grey skirt that denoted her uniform, but when he studied her like that—as if he were imagining her naked and willing in his bed—Anna felt as if there was nowhere to hide.

A trembling excitement soared through her blood at his near-insolent examination. An excitement that was like a gargantuan powerful wave dangerously poised to sweep her into uncharted waters she'd never dared visit before.

'In that case…I've had a change of heart,' Dante drawled, smiling. 'Maybe sharing my troubles with a sweet girl like you is just what I need tonight, Anna. What time do you finish?'

'Around midnight, by the time Brian and I have cashed up.' How was it possible for her voice to sound so level when inside a roaring furnace was all but consuming her?

'And how do you normally get home? Do you get a cab?'

'I live in, actually.'

Just like a popped balloon, her last defence deflated and it was no longer possible for her to pretend that the handsome, hard-jawed stranger hadn't affected her deeply. The truth was that he held a dangerous fascination for her. She was hypnotised by the simmering aura of sensuality implicit in his rough velvet voice and in the twin lakes of his troubled haunting eyes. As a result, her bones seemed to be held together by running water instead of strong connective tissue. Unable to think straight, Anna knew her returning glance was nervous as she gathered the round wooden tray up close to her chest as though it were a shield.

'Have you made up your mind about the drink? Only I've got to get back to the bar to work.'

'Another drink can wait.'

Unbuttoning his coat for the first time that evening, Dante handed her his empty glass with another long, slow, meaningful glance. His lean fingers brushed hers. *Did she imagine that they lingered there against her skin much longer than necessary?* His touch was like being grazed by lightning—deliberate or not.

'I'm staying here too tonight, Anna. And I think that we should have a drink together when your shift ends… don't you?'

A definite refusal was on the tip of her tongue, but inside the dogged belief clung that perhaps she really *could* help him by being a good listener. Her lips pursed tight to prevent it. But when she turned away it was as if some kind of aftershock from their encounter had seized her, because her limbs were shaking almost violently as she crossed the room to rejoin Brian…

There was no understanding such alternating and violent sweeps of emotion, thought Dante. He had just flown into London from his mother's funeral—the funeral of the one person in the world he had truly loved, who had always been there for him no matter what, who had been like a beacon of light he turned to when he ached to remember that beauty, grace and selfless kindness existed in the world.

Now that she was gone he was heartbroken…truly heartbroken. But another woman also occupied his thoughts right now. His body had somehow acquired a compelling desire to know the touch of a red-haired young witch with sherry-brown eyes that glinted beguilingly like firelight—a girl he had only just met whom he had all but mocked disparagingly when she'd shyly offered him a listening ear. Was it so rare that he met up with a genuinely nice girl that he had to punish her when he did?

His mother would turn in her newly dug grave! Bitterness and despair rising in his gorge, Dante ripped off his wristwatch to discard it onto the nearby polished side-table. His coat followed suit, but he let it fall care-lessly onto the bed instead. Several hundred dollars' worth of the finest cashmere—but what did it signify? His wealth had neither made him a better man nor a more generous one.

His personal assessment was brutally frank. All the businesses and property he had accumulated through mergers and acquisitions had demonstrated to him was how driven and ruthless he'd become. Yes, driven and ruthless—because of an underlying fear of losing it all. An impoverished childhood and a father who had deserted him had seen to that. He'd been so poor in the small mountain village in Italy where he'd grown up that his mother had been forced to earn their bread by dancing and singing for men in seedy bars in the nearby town, and Dante had long ago set his hungry intention for any career he might settle upon to make him wildly and disgustingly rich so that he might rescue them both.

His wealth would act as an insulating buffer between him and the rest of the world, he'd told himself. Then no one would have the chance to hurt him or his mother again, and neither would she have to humiliate herself by parading her beauty in front of men for money. Dante had carried that insulation with him into his marriage and into any other romantic relationship he'd briefly flirted with, forever seeking to protect his emotions. He'd become cold...not to mention a little heartless.

'No wonder they call you the ice man of the business world,' his American ex-wife, Marisa, had taunted him.

'You're so dedicated to the title that you even bring it home with you!'

At first his mother had been fiercely proud of his rocketing success. He'd bought her the house of her dreams in Lake Como, and made sure she always had plenty of money to buy whatever she wanted. But lately whenever he'd visited her she'd started to profess concern. With one failed marriage and a string of unhappy relationships behind him, it had only seemed to Renata that her son had lost all sense of priority.

It should be the people in his life who were important, she'd told him—not his business or the grand houses he bought—and if he continued in this soulless way then she would sell the richly decorated house on its exclusive plot by the lake and purchase a hut in the hills instead! After all, she'd been raised as a shepherd's daughter, and she wasn't ashamed to go back to where she'd begun even if *he* was. *Someone* had to show him what values were.

Dante grimaced at the hurtful memory of her distressed face and quavering voice when she'd said this to him in the hospital...

To diffuse his despair he deliberately brought his mind back to the titian-haired Anna Bailey. His reaction was purely male and instinctive, and his body tightened instantly. It was as though someone had stoked a fire beneath his blood and set it ceaselessly simmering. Reaching for his discarded watch, he impatiently scanned the time, all but boring a hole in the door with his naked, hungry glance as he waited for her to arrive—not once allowing himself to think that she *wouldn't*…

As if needing to enquire about something, her brooding new friend had leaned across the bar on his way out and whispered softly to Anna, *'Let's have that drink together in my room. I'm staying in the suite on the top floor. It would mean a lot to me…especially tonight. Please don't disappoint me.'*

His lips had been a hair's breadth away from her ear and his warm breath had all but set her alight. The seductive sensation had been the mesmerising equivalent of an intoxicating cocktail she was powerless to refuse. She knew it would make her dizzy and light-headed, but it still held a potent allure she couldn't ignore.

Anna had watched Dan's tall broad-shouldered physique as he left the bar with her heart thumping. Now, in the privacy of her room, she blew out a trembling breath, dropping down onto the padded stool in front of the dressing table because she hardly trusted her legs to keep her upright.

The enigmatic stranger was staying in the only suite in the building. It was the most luxurious and gorgeous accommodation she had ever seen. With its beautiful Turkish kelims hanging on the walls, artisan-created bespoke furniture and under-floor heating, no expense had been spared in its creation and it cost a small fortune to stay there for even *one* night.

Biting her lip, Anna peered into the dressing table mirror to gauge if her expression was as terrified as she felt. Was she really contemplating visiting a male guest in his room? Talking to that lovely couple who'd been to the theatre earlier, she had felt such a pang of envy at their closeness. It wasn't very often she succumbed to feelings of loneliness, but somehow tonight she *had*. What had he meant when he'd whispered, *It would mean a lot to me…especially tonight?* Was he feeling lonely too? Had the funeral she guessed he'd attended been for someone really close to him? His *wife* perhaps?

A heavy sigh, part compassion, part longing, left her. If anyone saw her go to his room then she really *could* lose her job. Was the loneliness that had infiltrated her blood tonight making her a little desperate? Not to mention reckless? Sighing again, Anna went into the bathroom to splash her face with cold water.

Back in the main room, she glanced unseeingly at the television that sat there. Somehow a late-night movie or talk show didn't hold any draw for her. Neither did curling up in bed alone with her thoughts appeal. She'd sensed an inexplicable overwhelming connection to the man who had whispered in her ear downstairs and it was somehow impossible to ignore it. Tomorrow he might be gone, she reasoned feverishly.

She would be wondering what might have been—and the feeling would gnaw away at her if she didn't act.

With fingers that shook, she freed her hair from the neatly coiled bun she'd got so adept at fashioning for work, then pulled a careless brush through the river of auburn silk that flowed down her back. Pinching her cheeks to make them pinker, she quickly changed into a dark green top and light blue jeans. He only wants to *talk*, she reassured herself as she walked out into the corridor. But her pulse beat with fright because he might have been looking for something more…something that in her heart of hearts she secretly longed for.

Flicking an anxious glance towards the small elevator that would soundlessly deliver her to the topmost floor, Anna sucked in a breath as she walked towards it.

The memory of Dan and his haunting mist-coloured eyes came back to her, cutting a swathe through her sudden doubt. Just because he was rich it didn't mean that he didn't suffer like everyone else…didn't mean that he didn't need help sometimes. And from her very first glimpse of him Anna had known he was tortured by something…

The polite welcome he'd intended got locked inside his throat when Dante opened the door to the vision that confronted him. She wore her bright auburn hair loose, and it resembled a burnished autumn sunset cascading down over her shoulders. His stomach muscles clamped tight and the saliva in his mouth dried to a sun-baked desert.

Finding his voice, he murmured, 'Come in.'

Stepping inside, Anna smiled. It was shy and brief, but it still gave him a jolt that had his heart thrumming with undeniable excitement.

'What can I get you to drink?' Moving across the gold and red Chinese rug that covered the main area of the polished wooden floor, Dante paused in front of the dark mahogany glass-fronted cabinet that contained several bottles of spirits behind it and rested his gaze on Anna.

'Nothing, thanks. Alcohol and me don't mix, I'm afraid. Just one sip is enough to make me dizzy.'

'A soft drink, then?'

'Please…just see to yourself. I'm fine, really.'

Dropping his hands restlessly to his hips, he let a rueful grin hijack his lips.

'I think I've probably had quite enough for one night.'

'You've decided not to drown your sorrows after all?'

'Not now that you've consented to visit me, Anna.'

She crossed her arms over her dark green top, and Dante couldn't think of a colour that would comple-ment her pale satin skin more. Without warning, the fresh, searing pain of his recent loss swept over him. It returned with renewed force and he wanted to reach out, anchor himself to life again, remind himself that even though his mother had gone beauty and grace were still his to appreciate if only he'd take the trouble to see it. If he brushed up close to such admirable qualities in Anna would it relieve him of the bitter, despairing thoughts that pounded on him so disturbingly? Thoughts that confirmed his growing belief that he must be no good?

Yes, his nature was clearly unlovable and unworthy of regard—hadn't his own father abandoned him?—so perhaps he deserved abandonment by the people close to him? Especially when he'd been so ruthlessly focused on making himself rich that he scarcely saw the needs of anyone else.

'It upsets me when you look like that,' Anna confessed softly.

'Like what?'

'As if you don't like yourself very much.'

'Is there no hiding from that all-seeing gaze of yours?' Dante retorted uncomfortably.

'I just want to help you if I can.'

'Do you? Do you really?'

'Of course I do. Why do you think I came? Would you like to talk about it?'

'No, sweetheart. Talking is *not* what I need right now,' he answered, gravel-voiced.

And for a man who had prided himself on achieving anything he put his mind to in life it was ironically too difficult a task to keep the raw need that surged through his body like a tidal wave completely out of his tone.

CHAPTER TWO

IN SLOW motion he reached for Anna's hand. His eyes—those intense, burning, ethereal eyes—held her willing prisoner, right then becoming her whole world.

'What do you want?' she whispered, hardly able to hear over the pounding of her heart. 'What do you need?'

'You, Anna…right now I want and need *you*.'

After that, words became unnecessary. His fingers were slipping through her hair, anchoring her head so that she was placed perfectly for his kiss when he delivered it…when the touch of his lips ignited a heartfelt need that had slumbered achingly inside her for years and promised to more than satisfy it.

She'd always thought that maybe her impassioned secret desires were doomed to remain unrequited. On the rare occasion when she'd allowed herself to overcome her mistrust and be caressed by a man, the experience had never remotely lived up to her hopes. All it had done was leave her feeling vulnerable, scared that she would end up alone and unloved until the end of her days. But now, as his warm velvet tongue so hungrily and devastatingly swept her mouth's interior, the flavours she tasted rocked her.

Along with passion, fervour and consuming need, Anna was alive to the anger, despair and pain that she tasted too. But she didn't let such stark emotions scare her…not when they mirrored feelings of her own that she'd often been too afraid to bring into the light. Because of that she innately understood the tumult that flowed heatedly through his blood—good *and* bad— even if she didn't know the details.

Crushed to his warm hard chest in its dark roll-necked sweater, she felt musky male heat and sexy woody cologne captivate her senses as he ravished her in the starved, insatiable way she'd always dreamt of being loved by a man. Holding on to his hard-muscled biceps to keep from falling, Anna feverishly and willingly paid him back in kind… And in her head echoed the advice from her mother that she'd never forgotten: *Only give yourself to someone you love…*

On the bed in a room where in their haste to be together they hadn't even paused to turn on a light they raided each other's clothes with trembling hands—desperate for skin on skin contact and more drugging open-mouthed kisses that promised to last all night long. And if he'd temporarily lost his mind in taking this young red-haired beauty to bed then Dante heartily welcomed the state. She was the first really good thing that had happened to him in ages, and he wasn't about to question his good fortune.

The intoxicating feminine scent of her body had already taken up residence in his blood, and it thrummed with wanting her. The arresting sight of that rippling blanket of fiery hair on the silk cream pillow behind her head made a stirring, ravishing picture that he would not soon forget. Now, as his hands eagerly caressed the smooth, slender contours of Anna's body, the breathless gasps she emitted made him blind to any other sensation but their wild and heady mutual desire. He was all but desperate to plunge inside her, to forget everything except the unrestrained thundering joy of the chemistry that had exploded between them from almost the first glance, to relegate the darkness that had recently threatened to suffocate him, to the shadows.

Sensing her stiffen a little as he explored her heat with his fingers, Dante rose up to cup and stroke her face. A duty that should have been at the forefront of his dazzled mind suddenly stabbed at his conscience.

'I'm sorry, Anna...I should protect you. Is that what you are concerned about?'

'It's okay,' she sighed, dark eyes shy. 'I'm protected already. I'm on the pill.'

For an indeterminate amount of time Dante got lost in her wide fire-lit stare, and then he came to and kissed her. The caress seemed to gentle her. Then, his blood flowing with increasing desire and demand, slowly, carefully, he drove himself deep inside her. The heat that exploded around him was incredible.

Anna's sherry-brown eyes smouldered and brightened at the same time, but Dante had not missed the momentary flash of apprehension in her beautiful glance either. Too aroused and aching to wonder about it for long, he felt his body naturally assume the age-old rhythm that would take him to the destination and release he longed for…a destination that could and *would* free him for a while from the merciless torment that had deluged him when his mother had breathed her last laboured breath in his arms. Instead of grief and misery, ecstasy and bliss would be his. And for a blessed short time, at least, all the hurt would be swept away…

His strength of purpose all but overwhelmed Anna as she watched him move over her, his arrow-straight hips slamming into hers as his loving became ever more intense, ever more voracious. By instinct and by desire she wound her long legs round his back, until he was so deep inside her that she felt as if her body no longer existed just as one. Instead, she and he had become a single entity, with two hearts beating wildly in tandem and mind, body and spirit in stunning accord. She had given herself to him without doubt that it was the right thing…*destined*, even.

Would it scare him to know that she thought that? A girl he had just met, to whom he probably wouldn't even give the time of day normally?

In the soft darkness that seemed to be growing ever

lighter as Anna's eyes grew more accustomed to it his smooth muscles rippled like warm steel beneath her trembling, caressing fingers. His breath was harshly ragged as he alternately devoured her lips and then, with that same hot, tormenting mouth, moved lower to caress her breasts. He suckled the rigid aching tips in turn, and Anna couldn't withhold the heated moan that broke free. It was as though her very womb rejoiced when he touched and caressed her.

When he rose up again to capture her lips in another hotly exploring and intimate kiss, something inside her started irrevocably to unravel, to spiral dizzyingly out of control. At first, because she was nervous of being so vulnerable and exposed in front of him, Anna tensed, trying to stem the sensation. But at that same moment she stared up at him, to find the corners of his oh-so-sensuous lips lifting in what might have well been a quietly knowing smile, and she completely gave up trying to control what was happening.

Instead, she allowed the fierce, elemental power of the tide that swept through her to take her where it willed. She was scarcely able to steal a breath as the heart-racing journey commandingly held sway. *It was like freefalling over a hundred-foot waterfall.* Feeling stunned, she didn't know if her mind or her heart raced more. Tears surged helplessly and she bit her lip to quiet the sounds that inevitably arose inside her throat.

Anna knew then that she was changed for ever by what had just occurred. Even her mother, with all her tenderly given advice, could not have prepared her for the powerful emotions that flooded her at surrendering herself to this man. Her gaze met his in genuine wonder. Moving even deeper inside her, his hard glistening body pinned her to the bed, keeping her there for long pulsating seconds. The blue-grey eyes that were so reminiscent of a restless stormy sea now scorched her as he silently surveyed her. The raw feeling and emotion he unwittingly revealed ripped achingly through Anna's heart.

Even though they were engaged in the most intimate act of all, he still seemed so isolated and alone. Like a lighthouse, with nothing but the sea surrounding it. She longed to be able to swim to him and reach him. But then, with an echoing shout that sounded as though it had been dragged up from the depths of his soul, a shudder went through him, and he stilled. Scalding heat invaded her.

'Anna...' he rasped, clasping her face between his hands and shaking his head as though she was an enigma he'd never resolve.

When he laid his head between her breasts, Anna rubbed away her tears and then enfolded him in her arms, stroking the impossibly soft fair hair almost as though he were a hurt child in need of love and care.

'It will be all right,' she soothed softly. 'Whatever's happened to make you so sad, it will pass given time. I truly believe that. One day soon you'll start to enjoy life again.'

'If you know that, then you have access to the kind

of faith that's a million light years away from where I am right now. And if my life runs true to form, it'll probably *stay* a million light years away.'

His warm breath skimmed her tender exposed skin like a lover blowing a kiss, while at the same time the shadow of beard covering his hard jaw lightly abraded her. But it was the utter desolation she heard in his gruffly velvet voice that disturbed Anna.

'You mustn't give up,' she urged, sliding her hands either side of his sculpted high cheekbones to make him look up at her.

Although he was surprised by her words, he couldn't disguise his anguish. 'Don't waste your reassurances on me, Anna. I'm okay. I'll survive... I always do.'

'You don't think life can be better than just surviving?'

'For you, angel, I hope it can be. You deserve it—you really do.'

'Sad things, bad things have happened to me too,' she offered shyly. 'Apart from childhood stuff. After a couple of years of doing jobs I hated I found one I really liked and excelled at. But I lost that post when some ruthless hotel magnate bought out my previous employers and installed his own staff. I didn't let myself be sad about it for long, though. I had no choice but to pick myself up and face the unknown. Luckily fate brought me here, to the Mirabelle. Sometimes help arrives when you most need it, you know?'

'Perhaps it does if your conduct has warranted it.'

'I wish you could tell me what's happened to make you feel so low. I thought—I thought perhaps because you were wearing black you might have just lost someone?'

Breathing silently for a while Dante didn't speak. Then he sighed. 'I already told you I'm not the unburdening kind. But I don't feel low right now, *cara*... How could I, lying here in your arms, hearing your heart beat beneath my cheek, having just enjoyed the pleasures and consolation of your beautiful body?'

Hot colour poured into Anna's cheeks. 'If I've brought you some comfort then I'm happy. But I think it's time I went. I really should get back to my room and get some sleep...I've got to make an early start in the morning.'

'So working in the bar isn't your only job?'

'No. I do a bit of everything. I'm learning the trade, so it's great. It's a small family-run hotel and we all muck in. In the mornings I'm a chambermaid.' She dimpled shyly.

'Stay.' Winding his fingers possessively round a spiralling length of her vivid burnished hair, Dante raised it tenderly to his lips. 'I want you to stay until morning. Would you do that for me, Anna? I can't promise you more than this one night, but I promise that I'll hold you close until the dawn comes up... If that's enough...if you're willing to accept just that...will you stay?'

Five years later

Anna flew into the large hotel kitchen, hurriedly unbuttoning her raincoat as she scanned the busy room for

Luigi, the head chef. Defying the stereotype that pro-claimed all good chefs should be on the large side, he was tall and thin, with a pointy chin and an abundance of curly black hair with threads of silver tied back in a ponytail. She found him straight away, the back of his chef's whites towards her as he weighed ingredients at one of the scrubbed steel counters, whistling an aria from a well-known opera.

'Did the produce arrive?' she asked breathlessly. 'I spoke to the manager at the deli and he told me it had already left in the van. Is it here?'

Turning round to acknowledge her, the first thing Luigi did was to look her up and down, then wag his finger. 'Have you eaten breakfast this morning? My guess is that you haven't, and yet you run around at a hundred miles an hour as if you can exist on fresh air alone!'

'As it happens I had a croissant at the deli while I was waiting to talk to the manager.'

Crossing her arms over her damp rain-spattered coat, Anna challenged him to disbelieve her. It was sweet that he took such an interest in her welfare and what she ate, but she was no longer the naive twenty-four-year-old she'd been when she first came to the hotel. She was thirty-two, in charge of her own destiny, and the assistant manager to boot!

'A croissant, eh? And how do you expect to survive on such a poor substitute for food as that until lunch-time? A croissant is nothing but air too!'

'It wasn't just air. It had apricot and custard in it, and it was extremely filling and very nice.' Sighing patiently, Anna let her rose-tinted lips naturally form a smile. 'Now, will you please answer my question about the produce delivery? Anita's expecting an important delegation for lunch today, and everything has to be just perfect.'

Luigi threw up his hands dramatically. 'And you believe it *won't* be? You should know by now that Luigi delivers nothing *but* perfection!'

'You're right. I do know that.'

'And, yes, the delivery has arrived—and the black olives are excellent as usual.'

'What a relief. So everything is fine, then? I mean, there aren't any problems?'

With her gaze swinging round towards Cheryl, who was the sous chef, and the three young kitchen assistants scurrying busily about the kitchen, Anna included them all in her question. She hadn't been made assistant manager without developing an ability to notice everything—from the mundane to the much more important—and she was very keen for all to be well.

Anita and Grant, the hotel's owners, had always prided themselves on running a tight ship, but an extremely friendly one too. They cared about their staff. That was why Anna had stayed on. And when she'd fallen pregnant they hadn't said she had to leave. Instead, the couple had been unstinting in their support of her, seeing her potential and insisting she occupy the

charming two-bedroom apartment in the basement of
the hotel as part of her remuneration for working there.
They had also helped her find a reliable and decent
local nursery for her baby, and encouraged her to take
an online management course with a view to promoting
her and helping her to earn a better salary. Consequently,
Anna was fiercely loyal as well as immensely grateful
to the couple.

'Everything's fine in the kitchen, Anna.' Cheryl
nodded, but then the slim, pretty blonde bit down anxiously on her lip and continued, 'Except we couldn't help
wondering why Anita and Grant had a delegation from
one of the most well-known hotel chains in the country
coming here for lunch. Can you tell us anything about
it?'

Anna's insides cartwheeled at the question. This afternoon the couple who owned the hotel had scheduled
a meeting with her to discuss something important, and
all last night and early this morning, as she'd got her
daughter Tia ready for kindergarten, she'd been fretting about what the subject might be. The charming
little hotel in its smart Georgian building was situated
in a very desirable corner of Covent Garden, but Anna
wasn't oblivious to the fact that the country was plunged
deep into a recession and reservations and consequently
takings were definitely down.

Were they going to be bought out by a more commercial hotel giant, and as a consequence would she lose

a job she loved again? And not just her job this time, but her home too? *It hardly bore thinking about.*

But now, seeing the obvious anxiety on not just Cheryl's but on the other staff members' faces too, she knew she had a duty to reassure them.

'To be absolutely honest with you I know nothing about it. My advice to you all would be to just concentrate on your work and not waste time on speculation. It won't help. If there's anything concerning us that we need to know, you can be sure we'll all get to hear about it soon. Now, I must get on. I've got to relieve Jason on Reception. He's standing in for Amy, who's phoned in sick.'

Time dragged interminably slowly as the hotel chain's delegation of three enjoyed the superb three-course lunch Luigi and his staff had prepared. Afterwards the two men and their female colleague were closeted in a meeting with Anita, Grant and their son Jason, the manager, for two and a half hours. Anna had never been a clock-watcher, but that afternoon she was.

It was a quarter to five by the time the phone rang on Reception to invite her into Jason's office for the promised meeting with him and his parents. In the meantime, Linda, the girl who did the late shift on the desk, had turned up, and now sat beside Anna powdering her nose.

Standing outside the manager's office, Anna smoothed her hands nervously down over her smart navy skirt, captured a stray auburn tendril that had come adrift from her ponytail, tucked it back into her *faux* ivory clip and then rapped briefly on the door. Greeted by three identically reassuring smiles, she nonetheless sensed immediately that all was not well.

'Dear Anna. Come and sit down, my love.'

The tiny brunette with the stylish elfin haircut, and the smooth, unlined face that belied the fact she was only a year away from the big sixty, welcomed her warmly, as usual.

'Firstly, you'll be pleased to know that the lunch Luigi prepared for our visitors today went extremely well. They were very impressed.'

'The man can certainly cook,' chipped in Grant, Anita's handsome silver-haired husband. 'You could almost forgive him for having an ego the size of an elephant!'

Anna immediately deduced he was nervous, and she perched on the edge of her seat, wishing her mouth wasn't suddenly so sickeningly dry, and that her stomach hadn't sunk as heavily as a giant boulder thrown into the sea. Searching for reassurance, her dark eyes met Jason's. The tall, slim young man whose features were a male version of his elfin mother's tried for a smile, but instead it came off as a resigned grimace. That was the moment when the alarm bells clanged deafeningly loud for Anna.

'So...' Her hands linking together nervously in her lap, she leaned forward even farther in her chair. 'What was the delegation from that commercial hotel chain doing here? Are we in trouble, or something?'

Anita started to speak, but Grant quickly took over.

'Yes, love.' He sighed, pulling a handkerchief out of his suit trousers to lightly mop his brow. 'Serious financial trouble, I'm afraid. Like many other small businesses, the recession's dealt us a heavy blow, and I'm sure you're aware that we've been losing money hand over fist. You've noticed how the reservations have fallen? It's really only the regulars that have stayed loyal to us. If we're to hold our own against some of the more popular hotels we need to reinvest and refurbish, but with the coffers practically empty, and banks refusing loans left right and centre, it's not likely to happen. Consequently, we've had no choice but to try and get some other form of help.'

'Does that mean that you're going to sell the hotel?' There was such a rush of blood to her head that Anna scarcely registered her boss's answer. All she could think of right then was Tia... How was she going feed and clothe her child if she lost her job? More urgently, where were they going to *live*?

'We were offered a buyout, but we haven't accepted the offer yet. We told the delegation that the hotel had been in the family for three generations and we needed some time to think things over.' Anita's usually sunny smile was painfully subdued. 'We have to get back to them by the end of the week. If we do agree to the buyout then unfortunately it means that none of us stay.

They'll want to refurbish and give the place their own look, run it with their own staff. I'm desperately sorry, Anna, but that's our position.'

She was struck silent by the news she'd just heard, but her mind was racing at a hundred miles an hour. Then, because she was also devoted to and protective of the interests of the family that had been so good to her and Tia, Anna forced a reassuring smile to her numbed lips.

'It's a difficult situation you're in,' she quietly acknowledged, 'and it's hardly your fault that there's a recession. The staff—including myself—will all eventually find other jobs, but what will you guys do? The hotel's been in your family for so long, and you love it...I know you do.'

'It's kind of you to be so concerned, love.' The big shoulders that strained Grant's suit jacket lifted in a shrug. 'I'm not saying it'll be easy, but we'll be fine. We've got each other, and that's what matters most in the end, isn't it...? The people you love, I mean.'

Not usually given to expressing his feelings in public, he squeezed Anita's hand. 'And we'll do whatever we can to help you find another flat, Anna. We certainly won't be walking out this door until we know you and Tia are safely settled somewhere. As for jobs... Well, with all the experience and qualifications you've gained these past few years, some grateful hotel will eagerly snap you up. You're a lovely girl and a complete asset... they'll quickly learn that.'

'So you'll let us all know by the end of the week what you've decided?'

'Perhaps sooner… Anita, Jason and I plan to spend the evening mulling things over. As soon as we've decided we'll let you and the rest of the staff know the decision we've reached.'

Getting to his feet, Grant sent Anna a friendly broad smile. 'It's five o'clock, and it's time you were running along to get that little angel of yours from aftercare at kindergarten, isn't it?'

Glancing down at the slim silver-linked watch on her wrist, Anna shot up from her seat. She hated to be late collecting Tia, and as always ached to see her child and learn about her day. Tonight, when she was in effect in limbo about their future, she would make an extra fuss of her, and hold her even tighter before putting her to bed.

CHAPTER THREE

STUDYING the sunlit view of the Thames from his Westminster apartment window, Dante suddenly moved impatiently away, jettisoning his mobile onto the bed. He'd just flown back from a business trip to New York, was feeling fuzzy-headed and tired, and yet the conversation he'd just had with a business friend of his had definitely acted like a triple dose of strong black coffee injected straight into his bloodstream.

The Mirabelle Hotel… It was a name he'd never forgotten. Even after five years. The family who owned it were apparently in dire straits financially, and had been forced to consider a buyout from the commercial hotel chain that his friend Eddie was on the board of. The place was situated in a prime location in central London, and as far as Eddie was concerned it should have been a done deal. But he'd just heard that the owners quite unbelievably rejected the offer. They had some old-fashioned notion that the business had to stay in the family, come what may.

Eddie had verbalised his astonishment at the number

of people who let their hearts rule their head in business. 'Will they ever learn? How about it, Dante?' he'd asked. 'Fancy giving it a shot? I don't doubt the place is a potential goldmine.'

He had ended the call after agreeing to meet with his friend for a drink later, but Eddie's parting remark had set Dante's mind racing. *That incredible night he'd stayed at that particular hotel had changed his life.* A veritable angel had motivated him to want to do some good in the world instead of just simply taking what he believed his hard work entitled him to. Not only had his aims become less ruthless and driven, but he had discovered a much more exciting avenue, and a way of doing business that far exceeded what he had achieved before in terms of personal satisfaction. It would definitely have had his mother cheering him from the sidelines if she'd lived to see the changes he'd made.

Although he was on the board of several blue chip companies, and still in mergers and acquisitions, Dante had sold off most of his businesses and now specialised in helping family-run concerns make their businesses more viable. He'd also reverted to his mother's surname, instead of the British one he'd adopted when he'd first started out in business here. Once again he was *Dante Romano*, and he had to admit it felt good to be much more authentic. Friends like Eddie still called him Dan, but that was okay. It was a fair enough shortening of Dante.

The Mirabelle Hotel…

Dante flopped down onto the king-sized bed with its opulent aubergine counterpane and picked up his phone. What had happened to the titian-haired beauty he'd spent the night with? Anna Bailey. The memory of her slid into his mind like the diaphanous caress of sensuous silk. *Closing his eyes, he could almost taste her.* He could even recall her perfume...something musky, with hints of orange and patchouli in it. It had been in her long flowing hair, and there had been traces on her milk-and-honey skin too.

His reflection deepening, Dante arrestingly recalled the sumptuously erotic, quivering pink mouth that he'd ached to plunder from almost the first moment he'd encountered it. The experience had been an utter revelation...as though it couldn't have been more right or perfect. For an endless-seeming moment he'd been dizzy with longing for her—his lovely lady of the night, who'd reached out to rescue him when all he could see ahead was blinding darkness.

His eyelids snapped open. Of all the businesses he could hear about that were in trouble...why the Mirabelle? One thing was certain—he couldn't let such an uncanny opportunity pass him by without at least checking it out...

She'd had another sleepless night. Duvet and pillow flung in frustration on the floor during the night. Her bed had become a taunting enemy instead of the safe, comforting haven she craved. And when she'd finally got up, Anna had uncharacteristically snapped at Tia as well.

As soon as she'd seen the child's luminous blue-grey eyes sparkle with tears across from her at the breakfast table, she'd immediately wanted to kick herself. Drawing the little girl urgently onto her lap, she'd kissed and hugged her and told her about a hundred times how sorry she was. Mummy didn't mean to shout. She was just a little bit stressed, she'd explained.

'What does *distressed* mean?' Tia had questioned, absently, playing with a long curling tendril of Anna's unbound auburn hair.

Perhaps her daughter had unwittingly stumbled upon the truth of what she was feeling? She *was* distressed.

'I'll explain when you come home from school, darling,' she'd hedged, praying the child would forget to ask. It wasn't something a four-year-old should be remotely acquainted with, to Anna's mind. Childhood should be joyful and carefree...*even if her own had been a million miles away from such an idyll.*

The Cathcarts had told Anna that they'd turned down the offer of a buyout from the big hotel chain. So when she'd entered the office the following morning to discover that her employers were considering a fresh offer—this one from an independent source who had been told about them by one of the delegation from the hotel chain—her insides had mimicked the nail-biting ascent and descent of a frantic rollercoaster ride for the second time. Once more the possibility of losing her job and home loomed worryingly large.

'Your parents said that an interested investor wants to help them improve profitability and modernise. Can you explain exactly what this means?' Anna had asked concernedly as she left the owners' office to walk with Jason to his.

'Don't look so worried, Anna. It's good news. Major investment is just what the Mirabelle needs. What we're hoping is that this guy will be interested enough to invest a large chunk of his own money in the business to help turn it around. He'll be the majority shareholder, but he won't own it outright. I've been checking out his record and it's quite impressive, to put it mildly. His interests are truly international, but his main concern is helping family-run businesses become more profitable. If we accept an offer from him to invest, it means that we stay running the hotel under his guidance and expertise. We'll have the chance to really take things to another level…even in the recession.'

Jason opened the door for Anna to precede him as they took their coffee into his cramped, cluttered office. Pushing some papers aside on a desk that scarcely had a corner free of paper debris, he left his mug of coffee on a stained cork coaster. An air of bubbling excitement underlaid his usually level tone.

'When he goes into a business with a view to help-ing it perform better,' he continued, 'he takes a good hard look at how it's being run and then advises on the changes that will make it more efficient and profitable. He particularly specialises in helping to resolve any conflicts that might be preventing people from working successfully together.'

Anna's brow creased. 'There aren't any conflicts amongst us, though, are there? Unless you mean Luigi's tendency to lord it over the others in the kitchen... They do get a bit fed up with him from time to time, but aren't all head chefs a bit like that? Egotistic and dramatic, I mean.'

'Generally I think that we all get on great. But that doesn't mean there isn't room for improvement.' As he paced the floor, it appeared as if Jason's enthusiasm was hard to contain. 'Unaired resentments can fester... we all know that. And this guy is a real people person. We thoroughly checked him out before inviting him over for a meeting. Apparently one of the first things he does is to interview everyone to discover how they feel about their job. He passionately believes that their attitude contributes to how well they work, and he has a unique reputation for getting staff and management to work more successfully together. The best thing of all is that the family get to stay doing what they love. We don't have to just sell up and go. Who knows? If the hotel starts to make a real profit, we might eventually be able to buy it back completely. The staff will remain too of course. It means you won't have to search for another job, Anna, isn't that great? Having someone like this Dante Romano guy invest his money in the hotel and take a look at how we can improve things could be the best opportunity we've had in ages!'

'And what's the pay-off for this man? I mean…what's in it for him besides making a profit? I doubt that he's going to do all this out of the goodness of his heart.'

She couldn't help it, but Anna wasn't entirely convinced. It all sounded too good to be true. Perhaps her nature wasn't as trusting as it could be, but then bruising experience had taught her to be alert to the glossily wrapped Christmas present that contained nothing but an empty shoebox.

The earnest dark-haired young man before her in the charcoal-grey suit that was showing signs of fraying at the edges of its cuffs abruptly stopped pacing.

'Of course there's a pay-off for him, Anna. He's a businessman! But his interest in helping us sounds perfectly genuine. I know you're only being protective of Mum and Dad but they're experienced hoteliers, don't forget. They won't agree to anything that remotely smacks of a scam or a rip-off. Yes, this guy might become the main shareholder—but he won't be running the business…*we* will. Plus, his policy is to take a longer-term view of situations, so he won't be in a hurry to just look at what he can get out of the business and then head for the hills.'

'You sound as though you believe this is the answer to all your family's prayers, Jason.'

It did indeed seem the ideal solution in terms of enabling them all to stay put, but Anna would rather hunt for another job and flat elsewhere if it meant that Grant and Anita wouldn't be out of pocket and the couple would have the means to start a good life again somewhere else. What if it really *was* in their best interests for them to sell the Mirabelle to a big commercial hotel giant?

'Nothing's been decided yet, Anna.' Compounding her guilt at being sceptical, Jason sounded subdued. 'But Romano is coming for lunch, and after he's eaten we'll have a proper meeting to thrash things out. Hopefully we'll be able to report back on what's been decided later on that afternoon. Would you mind going to talk to Luigi, to make sure he's got everything he needs to impress our visitor with his menu?'

'Of course.'

Carrying what remained of her half-drunk coffee to the door, Anna flashed him a smile to make up for her less than enthusiastic response earlier, but her stomach still churned at the prospect of the unknown changes that lay ahead for them all. She paused to glance back at the Cathcarts' preoccupied son, guessing that he probably saw the chance of working with this Romano chap as something that would enhance his reputation and ability—assets that were sometimes overshadowed by his much more confident and experienced father.

'I just want you to know that I'll do everything I can to help you and your parents, Jason. I love this hotel too, and I know it's been a very worrying time for all of you.'

'Thanks, Anna…I've always known I can count on you.'

The memories crashed in on Dante the instant he walked through the glass-panelled entrance into the cosily old-fashioned lobby, with its chintz armchairs and worn brown chesterfields.

After that incredible night with Anna he'd left the hotel in the early hours of the morning to jump in a cab and catch a flight to New York. His mother's death had plunged him into a tunnel of despair for a frighteningly long time. It had taken a good year or more for him to be able to function anywhere near normal again because, disturbingly, his work and everything he'd achieved had become utterly meaningless. Life had only started to improve when the warm memory of Anna's tenderness and his mother's unfailing belief that he was a much better man than the world suspected broke through the walls of his grief and his self-imposed isolation and helped him start to entertain the possibility of a very different, much more fulfilling future.

That was when Dante had decided to change his driven, selfish approach to something far more wholesome…

The Cathcarts were a delightful couple, with admirably solid values when it came to business and family. But Dante, although charmed by their unstinting hospitality and the superlative lunch, sensed that some of those solid values were a bit too entrenched in the past and needed to be brought up to date.

At lunch, his cool gaze assessed as much as it could as they talked, including the worn velvet hangings at the stately Georgian dining room windows, the tarnished silver cutlery and the slightly old-fashioned uniforms of the waiting staff. Afterwards he was invited to the Cathcarts' office to discuss the nuts and bolts of an investment.

As the fragrant, elegant Anita Cathcart poured him some coffee—at Dante's nod adding cream and sugar—he sat back in the comfortable leather chair, loosened his silk tie a little and relaxed. The hotel *was* in an absolutely prime location and could—as Eddie had foreseen—potentially be a goldmine. Because of lack of funds and the large debt they had accrued with the bank, it was clear the Cathcarts weren't able to make the best of their incredible asset, and that was where Dante came in.

'We'll get started soon, Mr Romano. We're just waiting for our assistant manager to join us. She's more like family than an employee, and we'd like her to be in on what we decide. She'll be along any minute now.'

Jason, the Cathcarts' slightly built son and manager, smiled diffidently at Dante as he sat down opposite him at the meeting table. He was clutching a pen and a spiral notebook and his hand shook a little. *What was the story with him?* Dante wondered. Was the manager's role too big an ask for him, or was it just that he struggled to assert himself under his parents' guardianship of the hotel?

'Was she informed about the meeting?'

'Yes…of course. It's just that she—'

'Then she should be here on time, like everyone else.'

His chastising glance encompassed them all, but Dante nonetheless tempered it with a trace of a smile. He heard the door behind him open and turned expectantly. A woman with hair the same hue as a bright russet apple stepped inside, bringing with her the faint but stirring scent of oranges and patchouli…

His thoughts careened to an abrupt halt…like a driver applying the emergency brake before hitting a wall. He stared in shock. *Anna…dear God, she still worked here?*

'I'm so sorry I'm late,' she breathed, porcelain skin flushing. 'I was—'

The startled leap in her sherry-brown eyes told Dante she recognised him. His heart—which had all but stalled—pumped a little harder as he realised he'd been genuinely afraid she might have forgotten him. *What a blow that would have been to his pride, when out of all the women he'd seen over the years she was the one that haunted him…*

'Mr Romano,' Grant Cathcart was saying, 'I'd like to introduce you to our stalwart assistant manager…Anna Bailey.'

Rising automatically to his feet, Dante extended his hand, praying hard that his voice wouldn't desert him. Anna's palm was fragile and slightly chilled as it slid into his. Their gazes locked as though magnetized, and though he sensed her tremble, inside he believed that he trembled *more*.

'Miss Bailey...I'm very pleased to meet you,' he heard himself announce.

'The feeling is mutual, Mr—Mr Romano,' she replied politely.

Her warm velvet voice bathed his senses in liquid honey. Arresting memories of their unforgettable night together came pouring back in a disturbing heated rush. Realising that his hand still covered hers, Dante reluctantly withdrew it.

'Why don't you come and sit down, Anna love?' Anita invited. 'There's plenty of coffee in the pot if you'd like some.'

'I'm fine, thanks,' Anna murmured distractedly.

As Dante watched her, she moved like a sleepwalker to a seat at the opposite side of the table, next to Jason, and he didn't miss the spark of warmth in the other man's dark eyes as he silently acknowledged her. *Was something going on there?* A hot flash of jealousy hit Dante a glancing blow as he resumed his seat.

'Well, if everybody's ready, we'll make a start, shall we?' With a respectful glance in their visitor's direction, Grant Cathcart organised his notes and prepared to address the meeting.

* * *

Dante Romano. No wonder she'd never been able to find him! What had instigated the name-change? she wondered. Underneath, was he still as ruthless and cutthroat as it had said in the newspaper reports she'd read when she'd been searching for him? But what did it matter when it had already been decided by the Cathcarts that he was going to be their saviour?

As well as investing a substantial amount of money in the Mirabelle, Dante Romano was taking the hotel, its owners and its staff firmly under his wing. Being satisfied that Anita and Grant were completely happy with the arrangement was one thing. *Only time would tell if Anna would be equally happy.* There was a very big—in fact a *huge* hurdle she had to cross before then.

Shaking her head, she emitted a small groan as she added chopped up red and green peppers to the stir-fry she was busy cooking for herself and Tia.

She'd half believed she was hallucinating when she'd walked into the office to find Dan, or *Dante* as he called himself now, sitting there. And she'd had such a jolt when his incredible winter-coloured eyes had bored into hers. In those electrifying few seconds the world could have ended, and she hadn't been able to drag her hypnotised gaze away.

Five years ago she'd never even asked him his full name. When he'd asked her to stay with him for the night but not to expect anything more she'd agreed— and she'd promised herself she wouldn't speculate on where he would go or what he would do when he left her, even if it ultimately meant he was going from her arms to someone else's.

Consoling herself that she'd helped comfort him in his hour of need, and that no matter how emotionally painful it was it would have to be enough, Anna had never intended to try and track him down afterwards. But when she'd found herself pregnant with his child she'd reasoned that she owed it to him to let him know. However, discovering that the suite's occupant Dan Masterson was a veritable 'shark' in the world of international business, who didn't care who he brought down in his empire-building quest, had definitely given her pause. He might have been tender with Anna that night they'd spent together, and he might have been troubled, but could she knowingly risk inflicting such a driven ruthless man on her child?

She'd decided *no*, she couldn't. Besides, she'd definitely received the impression from her one-night lover that he wasn't interested in a relationship, so why would he be interested in the fact that he'd left his one-time-only lover pregnant? she'd reasoned.

Leading up to that night five years ago she'd been working so hard, what with all the different jobs she did at the hotel—sometimes even working double shifts back to back—and because she'd been extremely tired, she'd absent-mindedly forgotten to take one of her daily contraceptive pills. It had only dawned on Anna to check when early-morning nausea had become a worrying recurrence.

Some months after Tia had been born she'd revised her decision not to get in touch with Dan and decided to try once more to locate him. *It had been as though he had vanished.* The only information about him she'd been able to glean was stuff from the past. There had been nothing to indicate what he was doing nearly eighteen months after they'd met.

From the living room came the delighted chuckle of her small daughter as she knocked down the building blocks she'd had as a toddler that she'd been happily shaping into a wobbling tower for the past ten minutes or so. A wave of sadness and terror deluged her mother all at once. What would Dan—or Dante, as she should call him now—think when he found out that their passionate night together all those years ago had made him a father? How poignant that he hadn't had the privilege of knowing his own delightful daughter. Anna had no doubt that it would have enhanced his life in a myriad different ways. But what could she have done when it had seemed as though he didn't exist any more?

With genuine regret she squeezed her eyes shut, then quickly opened them again. Her terror came from the fact that she knew he was a very rich and influential man indeed—rich enough to invest in a major share of the hotel that was the means of her employment and her place to live. How would it reflect on Anna if Dante's was the controlling share? What if he decided she wasn't up to her job—or, worse still, that he wanted to try and take Tia away from her? A man as wealthy as him must have access to all kinds of power…particularly *legal* power.

Abruptly switching off the burner beneath the wooden-handled wok, Anna wrapped her arms protectively round her middle as she crossed the tiled kitchen floor to examine the collage of baby and toddler photographs of Tia that were framed on the wall there. Behind her, the suddenly ringing telephone made her jump.

'Hello?'

'Anna? It's me—Dante. I'm still in the hotel. You rushed off rather quickly after the meeting and I think we need to talk. I believe you have a flat downstairs— can I come down and see you?'

CHAPTER FOUR

ANNA was struck dumb by Dante's request. What should she do? If she agreed for him to come down to the flat, how to prepare him for her news when Tia was there, large as life, playing happily in the living room? There was no time to prepare for anything!

'I'd love to talk to you—I really would—but—'

'But?'

She could imagine him sardonically curling his lip. He knew she was hedging. God, why couldn't she be a better actress?

'I'm making dinner at the moment. Why don't we arrange to meet up tomorrow? You're coming in to start working with Grant and Anita, aren't you?'

'I think I'd rather come and talk to you right now, Anna. I'll be with you in about five minutes.'

He put down the phone. Anna was left staring at the receiver in her hand as if it was a grenade she'd just pulled the pin from.

'Tia, we're going to have a visitor in a minute. We'll have dinner after he's gone, okay?'

She sped round the compact living room, sweeping up strewn toys into her arms like a whirlwind, then throwing them onto the end of the faded gold couch as if she was aiming to knock down coconuts at a carnival stall. When Dante arrived she would hide her emotions as best she could, she promised herself, yanking her oversized emerald sweater further down over her hips. Yes, she would hide behind her assistant manager's mask—be unflustered and professional, as if she could totally handle whatever he cared to throw at her. No matter that she hadn't been able to so much as *look* at another man since he'd left, because her heart had been irrevocably stolen by him.

She didn't have a hope of concealing her feelings behind a managerial mask under the circumstances. How could she?

'Who's coming to see us, Mummy?' Feeling a tug on her trouser-leg, Anna's gaze fell distractedly into her daughter's. The child's big blue-grey eyes—eyes, she realised with another frisson of shock, that were *identical* to her father's—were avid with curiosity. 'Is it Auntie Anita?'

'No, darling. It's not Auntie Anita.' Chewing anxiously down on her lip, Anna forced herself to smile. 'It's a man called Dante Romano and—and he's an old friend of mine.'

'If he's your friend, why haven't I seen him before?' Tia's husky little voice was plaintive.

'Because—'

The knock on the hallway door just outside completely silenced whatever it was that Anna had been about to say. Rolling up her sweater sleeves, she reached for Tia's hand and led her as calmly as she was able over to the couch, where she sat her down. Crouching in front of her, she tenderly stroked back some golden corkscrew curls from her forehead.

'Don't be nervous, will you? He's—he's a very nice man, and I'm sure he'll be very pleased to meet you.'

As she hurried out into the hallway a surge of irrepressibly strong emotion made tears flood into her eyes. Not now! she moaned silently, wiping them away with the back of her hand. *Why don't you wait to hear what he has to say before you start crying?*

'Hi.' His handsome smile was devastatingly confident, and Anna could scarcely contain the anger that suddenly rose up inside her, let alone analyse it.

'Hello,' she murmured in reply, praying he wouldn't see the evidence of her tears. 'Come in.'

Had he called at a bad time? Dante speculated. Her beautiful brown eyes appeared slightly moist. He guessed she would rather have put off his visit until tomorrow, but the fact of the matter was he couldn't wait until then to see her and talk to her again. Ever since Anna had walked into that office he'd ached to get her alone, find out what she'd been doing all these years… maybe even ask if she'd ever thought about him since that extraordinary night they'd spent together.

Folding her arms, she stood squarely in front of him,

leaving him with the distinct notion he wasn't going to be invited in any farther. Fighting down the sense of rejection that bubbled up inside him, he swept his glance hungrily over her pale oval face. The dazzling fire-lit brown eyes were wary, he noticed, and the softly shaped mouth that was barely glazed with some rasp-berry-coloured lipgloss was serious and unsmiling.

'You said you wanted to talk…what about?'

It wasn't a very promising start. Apprehension flooded into the pit of Dante's stomach.

'What a greeting. You make it sound like you're ex-pecting an interrogation.' He shrugged, momentarily thrown off balance by her cool reception.

'It's just that I'm busy.'

'Cooking, you said?' He quirked a slightly mocking eyebrow and sniffed the air.

'Look…how do you expect me to greet you after all this time? The truth is you're the last person I ever expected to see again! For you to show up now, because you're the new investor in the Mirabelle, is obviously a shock…a shock that I was totally unprepared for.' Pursing her lips, she was clearly distressed. 'I don't know how to put this any other way, Mr Romano, and please don't think me presumptuous, but I think that whatever else happens round here our relationship should remain strictly professional for as long as we have to work together.'

'Why? Afraid you might be tempted to instigate a repeat performance of the last time we got together?'

Stung by her aloof air, and the distance she seemed so eager to put between them, Dante said the first thing that entered his head. Trouble was, he'd be *lying* if he said the thought of them being intimate *hadn't* crossed his mind. It was practically all he'd been dwelling on since setting eyes on her.

Blushing hard, Anna gazed down at the floor. When she glanced up at him again her dark eyes were spilling over with fury.

'What a hateful, arrogant thing to say! Bad enough that you only thought me good enough for a one-night stand, but to come here now and assume that I—that I would even—' She gulped in a deep breath to calm herself. 'Some of us have moved on.'

Dante nodded, sensing a muscle flex hard in the side of his cheek. 'And you *have* moved on, haven't you, Anna? Assistant Manager, no less.'

'If you're suggesting I got the position by any other means than by damned hard work then you can just turn around and leave right now. I certainly don't intend to meekly stand here while you mock and insult me!'

His lips twitched into a smile. He couldn't help it. Did she have any idea how sexy she was when she was angry? With that fiery-red hair spilling over her shoulders and those dark eyes flashing…it would test the libidinous mettle of any red-blooded heterosexual male. To Dante it felt as if a lighted match had been dropped into his blood, and it had ignited as though it were petrol.

'I didn't come here to insult you, Anna. I merely wanted to see you again in private…that's all.'

'I heard you shouting, Mummy.'

A little girl with the prettiest corkscrew blond curls Dante had ever seen suddenly emerged from a room along the hall. Deep shock scissored through him. She'd addressed Anna as 'Mummy'.

Definitely flustered, Anna ran her fingers over the child's softly wayward hair, captured a small hand in hers and squeezed it.

'Tia…this is the man I told you about. Mr Romano.'

'Why are you calling him Mr Romano when you told me his name was Dante?'

The girl was engagingly forthright. Dante smiled, and the child dimpled shyly up at him.

'Hello, Tia.' Staring into her riveting misty-coloured eyes, he frowned, not knowing why she suddenly seemed so familiar. Quickly he returned his attention to Anna. 'You got married and had a child?' he said numbly. 'Was that the "moving on" you referred to?'

'I'm not married.'

'But you're still with her father?'

Her cheeks pinking with embarrassment, she sighed. 'No…I'm not.'

'Obviously things didn't work out between you?' Dante's racing heartbeat started to stabilise. So she was alone again? It must have been tough, raising her child on her own. He wondered if the father kept in touch and assumed the proper responsibility for his daughter's welfare. Having had a father who had shamelessly deserted him and his mother when it didn't suit him to be responsible, Dante deplored the mere idea that the man might have turned his back on Anna and the child.

'Perhaps—perhaps you'd better come in after all.' Saying no more, Anna turned back towards the room along the hallway, Tia's hand gripped firmly in hers.

Barely knowing what to make of this, Dante followed. The living room was charming. The walls were painted in an off-white cream-coloured tone, helping to create a very attractive sense of spaciousness and light. It was the perfect solution in a basement apartment where the long rectangular windows were built too high up to let in much daylight.

'Please,' she said nervously, gesturing towards a plump gold-coloured couch with toys strewn at one end, 'sit down. Can I get you something to drink?'

She'd gone from hostile to the perfect hostess in a couple of seconds flat. It immediately made Dante suspicious. He dropped down onto the couch.

'No, thanks.' Freeing his tie a little from his shirt collar, he gave Tia a smile then leant forward, his hands linked loosely across his thighs. 'What's going on, Anna? And don't tell me nothing… I'm too good a reader of people to buy that.'

She was alternately twisting her hands together and fiddling with the ends of her bright auburn hair. The tension already building in Dante's iron-hard stomach muscles increased an uncomfortable notch.

'Tia? Would you go into your bedroom for a minute and look for that colouring book we were searching for earlier? You know the one—with the farm animals on the front? Have a really good look and bring some crayons too.'

'Is Dante going to help me colour in my book, Mummy?' The little girl's voice was hopeful.

'Sure.' He grinned at her. 'Why not?'

When Tia had left them to run along the hallway to her bedroom, Anna's dark eyes immediately cleaved apprehensively to Dante's. 'That night—the night we were together...' She cleared her throat a little and his avid gaze didn't waver from hers for a second. 'I got pregnant. I didn't lie when I told you I was on the pill, but because I'd been working so hard I missed taking one... Anyway...Tia's yours. What I'm saying—what I'm trying to tell you—is that you're her father.'

He'd heard of white-outs, but not being enamoured of snow or freezing weather had never experienced one. He imagined the blinding sensation of disorientation that currently gripped him was a little like that condition. Time ticked on in its own relentless way, but for a long moment he couldn't distinguish anything much. Feelings, thoughts—they just didn't exist. He quite simply felt numb. Then, when emotions started to pour through him like a riptide, he pushed to his feet, staring hard at the slender redhead who stood stock-still, her brown eyes a myriad palette of shifting colours Dante couldn't decipher right then.

'What are you up to?' he demanded. 'Has someone put you up to this to try and swindle money from me? Answer me, damn it!' He drove his shaking fingers through his hair in a bid to still them. 'Tell me what you just said again, Anna—so I can be sure I didn't misunderstand you.'

'Nobody put me up to anything, and nor do I want your money. I'm telling you the truth, Dante. That night we spent together resulted in me becoming pregnant.'

'And the baby you were carrying is Tia?'

'Yes.'

'Then if that's the truth, why in God's name didn't you find me to let me know?'

'We agreed.' She swallowed hard. Her flawless smooth skin was alabaster-pale, Dante registered without sympathy. 'We agreed that we wouldn't hold each other to anything...that it was just for the one night and in the morning we'd both move on. You were—you were so troubled that night. I knew you were hurting. I didn't know what had happened, because you didn't tell me, but I guessed you might have just lost someone close. You weren't looking for anything deep...like a relationship. I knew that. You didn't even tell me your last name. You simply wanted—*needed* to be close to someone and for some reason—' She momentarily dipped her head. 'For some reason you chose me.'

Barely trusting himself to speak, because his chest

felt so tight and he was afraid he might just explode, Dante grimly shook his head.

'You could have easily found out my last name by checking in the reservations book. From there you could have found a contact address. Why didn't you?'

She hesitated, as if she was about to say something, but changed her mind. 'I—I told you. I didn't because we'd made an agreement. I was respecting your wishes… that's all.'

'Respecting my wishes? Are you crazy? This wasn't just some simple mistake you could brush aside, woman! Can't you see what you've done? You've denied me my own child. For over four years my daughter has lived without her father. Did she never ask about me?'

'Yes…she—she did.'

'Then what did you tell her?'

Her expression anguished, Anna was clearly struggling to give him a reply.

'When Tia asked me why her daddy wasn't around I—I just told her that you'd been ill and had to go away to get better. What else could I tell her when I had no idea where you were or even if you'd care?'

Lifting a shaky hand to his forehead Dante grimaced painfully. 'And whose fault is that, when you couldn't even be bothered to find me?'

Her skin turned even paler. 'I understand why you'd want to blame me, but at the time the decision not to see each other again was ostensibly *yours*, if you remember?'

'And while I've been relegated to the back of your mind as some past inconvenient mistake…has there been anyone else on the scene?' Dante demanded, his temper flashing like an electrical storm out of a previously calm summer sky. 'Another man who's played father to Tia?'

'No, there hasn't. I've been raising her on my own, and at the same time trying to build a career so that I can support us both. I don't have time for relationships with other men!'

This last statement had clearly made her angry. The tightness in Dante's chest eased a little, but not much. He was still furious with her. Frankly, the idea that his child might have witnessed a parade of different men filing through her mother's life filled him with horror and distress. Children needed stability, support, *love*… The thought brought him up short. He had accepted without dispute the fact that Tia was his daughter—accepted the word of a woman he had only known for one too short and incredible night. Yet the moment he had gazed into Tia's eyes—eyes that were the same unusual light shade as his—Dante had somehow known that she belonged to him.

'Well, now you *will* make time for a relationship, Anna. Your comfortable little idyll of having things just the way you want them is about to change dramatically. You've dropped the bombshell that I am father to a daughter, and now you will have to accept the consequences.'

'What consequences?' The colour seemed to drain out of her face.

'What do you think?' Dante snarled, his hands curling into fists down by his sides. 'What do you think will happen now that I know I fathered a child that night? Did you think I would calmly walk away, saying, *"Oh, well"*? From this moment on I fully intend to be a father to our daughter, and that means I want a legalised relationship with you—her mother. Purely for the child's sake, you understand, and not because it fills me with joy to be with you again, Anna! Not after the terrible deceit you have played on me. So, no... I won't be calmly walking away so that you can happily continue the way you were. It's not just the hotel that will undergo a great change now that I am here.'

'I won't prevent you from playing an important part in Tia's life now that you know the truth...if that's what you want,' Anna replied quietly, though her expression mirrored a silent plea, 'but we don't need to be in a relationship for that. Five years ago you made it very clear that you weren't interested in taking things any further. I accepted that. I've made a good life for myself working at the hotel. The owners have been more than kind to me and Tia, and I'm extremely grateful to them for all they've done. As far as I can see there's no need for that arrangement to change.'

Rubbing his fingers into his temples, Dante breathed out an impatient sigh. He didn't like referring to the past, but in this case he would have to.

'Five years ago I was bordering on burn-out from working too hard and too long…then my mother died. She was Italian. The name I use now is my proper full name—the name my mother gave me. I only mention it because the night we met I'd just flown back from her funeral in Italy. I was living in New York at the time, but I couldn't get a direct flight back there so made a stopover in London for the night. Having just been bereaved, I was hardly in a fit state to contemplate a relationship with anyone. But, like you with Tia, my mother raised me on my own as a single parent, and I saw first-hand how hard life was for her. It made her old before her time, and I worried about her constantly. I'll be damned if I'll visit that hurtful existence on my own child. That being the way things stand, you have no choice but to enter into a relationship with me—a relationship that can have only one destination… Our marriage.'

Sympathetically examining the compellingly hand-some face with those searing stormy eyes—the face that she had fantasised over and dreamed longingly about for five long, lonely years—Anna willed her emotions not to get the better of her. She was gratified to hear at last an explanation as to why Dante had appeared so haunted and troubled that night, and for the second time in their association her heart went out to him. But while she understood the fears that their own situation must be raising inside him, because he too had been brought up without a father, she balked at the idea of tying herself to him merely for convenience. Dante Romano might be the father of her beloved daughter, but he was still an unknown quantity to Anna. It would be nothing less than reckless to marry him—even though privately she still held a torch for him and always would.

'I'm really sorry that you lost your mother, Dante. I could see at the time how devastated you were. But I won't be told I'm going to have to marry you just because you're Tia's father. That would be crazy. We don't even know each other. And for your information I don't want to marry anyone. I'm happy just as I am, doing my job and taking care of Tia. I won't stop you from being in her life—I'd be glad of it, if that's what you honestly want. But, like I said before, you and I don't have to be in a relationship for that.'

'Like hell we don't!' He scowled at her.

'And there's one more thing.' Feeling nervous, and knowing she was on shaky ground already, Anna rubbed a chilled palm down over her sweater. 'I'd be grateful if you didn't say anything to Grant and Anita about us knowing each other...at least not yet. It's such an awkward situation, and I *will* tell them, but I need some time to think about how best to broach the subject. Please do this one favour for me, and I promise I'll tell them soon.'

'I'll let you off the hook for a couple of days,' Dante agreed reluctantly. 'But then you *will* be telling them, Anna—about us *and* Tia. You can be absolutely sure about that.'

'I found my colouring book and my crayons!' Rushing back into the room like a tiny blond cyclone, Tia blew out a happy breath and headed straight for Dante.

For a moment he stood stock-still, his lean, smartly suited figure apparently all at sea. Anna realised that, like her, he was desperately trying to get his emotions under control. *Put yourself in his shoes*, she told herself. How would you feel if you were suddenly confronted with the astonishing fact that you'd fathered a child? A child you hadn't even known existed up until now?

'Will you help me colour in my book, please?'

The tall broad-shouldered man whose dark blond hair was slightly mussed from his agitated fingers had let Tia pierce his heart with her big soulful eyes, Anna saw. Her teeth clamped down on her lip, but it didn't stop them from trembling.

'I promised I would, didn't I?' she heard Dante agree huskily, and then he slipped his hand into his daughter's and allowed her to lead him back to the couch. Before he sat down, he shucked off the dark blue exquisitely lined jacket of his business suit, throwing it carelessly onto the cushions.

His arresting light eyes met Anna's. 'I'd like that drink you offered earlier after all,' he commented. 'Coffee would be good. I take it with milk and two sugars, thanks.'

CHAPTER FIVE

BY THE time Dante was ready to leave that evening—
having accepted Anna's invitation to join them for dinner—Tia was completely besotted with the man.

Although Anna's senses had been minutely attuned to
the fact that the man she had so recklessly given herself
to that magical night five years ago was now sitting opposite her at her dining table there had been no struggle
to make awkward conversation. Not when her daughter
had chatted enough for them both. So engaged had she
been with Dante's company that for the first time ever
she'd protested loudly about going to bed. She had only
agreed to go if Dante would read her a bedtime story—
which he duly had.

When he'd emerged from her bedroom half an hour
later his air had been subdued and preoccupied. It had
been obvious that he was trying hard to come to terms
with a situation he probably couldn't have envisaged
in a thousand years. After all, Anna had told him she
was on the pill, so what need had there been for him to
worry?

Assuming he would want to discuss things further, she'd risked giving him a smile, but he had shown no inclination to linger…the opposite, in fact. How was she supposed to confess that she wasn't as heartless as he'd assumed, and that she *had* planned to let him know about her pregnancy, but when she'd discovered his ruthless reputation in the business world she'd been scared that when the baby was born he might try and take him or her away from her? Then, when she'd tried again later, it had been as though 'Dan Masterson' had simply vanished off the radar.

'We've got a long day of discussion and planning about the hotel tomorrow,' he said to her now. 'There'll be plenty of time after work in the evening for us to discuss our personal situation in more depth.' There was a fierce glint in his eyes that said *do not doubt that*. 'For now I'll say goodnight, *innamorata*, and I will see you in the morning. Sleep well. You're going to need to be doubly alert for all we have to face tomorrow,' he added, a dark blond eyebrow lifting a little mockingly even though his voice and manner was still distant and aloof.

Innamorata—didn't that mean *sweetheart* in Italian? Anna shivered hard. Having asserted that she wasn't interested in a relationship, she wondered if Dante would still adhere to his insistence that they marry? A tug of uncertainty mingled with the faintest of faint hopes in the pit of her stomach. *What if he concluded that his association with Tia was the only one that really counted?*

A lonely feeling crept over her. And when she was still lying awake in the early hours of the morning because she couldn't get Dante out of her mind, Anna seriously worried how on earth she was going to get through her working day without at some point falling asleep on the job.

Reflecting on the new partner's all-business tone when he'd left, as well as his warning that she needed to be 'doubly alert', she imagined that would go down like the proverbial ton of bricks. It certainly wouldn't reveal her at her best. And as for the news he had just so shockingly learned…would Dante be so angry with her for not revealing his daughter's existence to him that he would try to punish her in some way? For instance, would her job and her home be under threat now that he was in the driving seat?

Thumping her pillow in pure frustration, Anna released a pained groan. Then, with her eyes determinedly shut, she sent up a swift plea to the universe for the incessant worry going through her mind to grind to a halt so that she might at least get a couple of hours' rest before having to rise for work…

'You're late, Miss Bailey.'

The clipped pronouncement came not from the owners of the hotel, nor Jason their son, but from Dante. He was seated at the head of the meeting table in Grant and Anita's office, wearing another mouthwateringly tailored dark suit that he'd teamed with an elegant black shirt—the only splash of colour came from his vivid cobalt silk tie and his disturbing light eyes…eyes that now pierced Anna like the dazzling beams of sunlight reflecting on water as she stood in the doorway, wrestling with her embarrassment at being reprimanded.

So the gloves were off, were they? Clearly he'd reflected on her news of yesterday and he *did* mean to punish her. Making it clear he was the one in charge, he'd probably make her rue the day she'd kept Tia a secret from him and then had the temerity to say she wouldn't marry him.

'I'm sorry. I'm afraid I had a bit of a sleepless night. When I did manage to drop off I ended up sleeping through the alarm.'

'Tia's not coming down with something, is she?' Anita's perfectly arched brows lifted concernedly.

Straight away, Anna saw Dante's smooth lightly-tanned forehead tighten too.

'No, she's fine. I just couldn't sleep, that's all.'

Frown disappearing, he scanned a document in front of him on the table, then lifted his gaze to examine her coolly. 'That kind of lame excuse for being late is unacceptable, Miss Bailey. I'd advise you to get a louder alarm clock if you want to keep your position here.'

Even her employers' mouths dropped opened at that. As the avuncular Grant shifted uncomfortably in his seat, Anita directed a sympathetic smile at Anna and mouthed *don't worry.*

'Dante?'

The older woman moved her attention immediately back to the outrageously handsome man at the head of the table. Although her voice was soft it didn't lack authority.

'Sleeping through the alarm happens to the best of us from time to time—and we've always called our staff by their first names…especially Anna. As we indicated to you before, she's not just an employee. She's a friend too.'

'And that's precisely what goes wrong in family businesses,' Dante returned, sharp as a blade. 'Whilst I'm all for informality, to a degree, it's still important to monitor it so it doesn't get out of control, or your staff will start taking advantage of your goodwill.'

'How dare you?' With her heart beating a tattoo that wouldn't shame a military marching band, Anna glared at the owners' new partner and took affront at the superior tone in his voice. 'I would never dream of taking advantage of my employers' goodwill. I owe them everything…they've given me a job, a home—'

Pulling out a chair next to Jason and dropping down into it, she firmly closed her lips to stop any further angry words from recklessly pouring out. What was between Dante and her was personal, she thought furiously. She wouldn't drag her personal resentments into work meetings and neither should he!

So she hadn't been able to sleep last night? Dante reflected with satisfaction, ignoring her outburst. His glance swept helplessly over her delicate, now flushed features. Well, neither had he. Learning only a few short hours ago that he was the father of the most engaging and beautiful child he'd ever seen had never been going to help him get the best night's rest known to man. Neither was the fact that Anna had seemed far from keen on the idea of marrying him. *As in the past, rejection was like a scythe, slicing open his heart.* But Dante had already decided she could refuse him all she liked—because in the end he was determined to have his way. As far as his daughter was concerned he would use any means possible to ensure she had the upbringing and the future she deserved. But right now he needed to deal with what was in front of him—his promise and commitment to the Mirabelle, to turn the business around and have it flourishing again. Already his mind was buzzing with ideas for changes and improvements. And he would begin as he usually began when he went into a business to update it and improve its profitability—he would interview the staff…

'Can I pour you some coffee?' Reaching for the newly filled cafetière, Dante glanced expectantly at Anna as she sat down on the other side of his desk.

'No, thank you.' Her sherry-brown gaze briefly acknowledged him then quickly moved away again.

Irritation and disappointment threatened his effort to

be as good-humoured and fair as possible. Was she still brooding about him ticking her off earlier? As much as his pride wanted to cajole her into viewing him more favourably, right now this interview needed to get underway as well as remain professional, and Dante knew a battle of wills wouldn't help. Their personal issues would have to wait until later tonight.

'Fine… Good. We'll make a start, then, shall we?'

'As you wish.'

'For goodness' sake, you don't have to sit there like you're about to climb the steps up to the guillotine! All I'm doing is interviewing you about your job.' Tunnelling his fingers through his hair, Dante knew his breath was slightly ragged as he fought to regain control of his temper. What was it about this woman that always inflamed him? Whether it was lustful desire or a burst of bad temper she always seemed to inspire some kind of volatile reaction.

'Am I going to keep my job, or are you planning to replace me with someone else in your clean sweep?'

'What?' His dark blond brows drew together in puzzlement. Anna was slumped back in her chair, and the fear in her eyes was suddenly clear as daylight to Dante.

'I mean, in your drive to improve things, is my job under threat?'

A flash of memory of that night they'd met came back to Dante, and he recalled her telling him that she'd lost her previous job to a 'ruthless takeover'.

'I'm only interviewing you to find out what your responsibilities and duties are, and if you enjoy your work. I have no plans to replace or fire anyone right now, so your job is quite safe.'

'Oh...' Her sigh was relieved. Her restless hand lifted to play with the tiny heart-shaped crystal on the end of a slim gold chain she wore round her neck. *Had an admirer bought her that?*

His equilibrium coming under disagreeable fire yet again, Dante leaned forward to level his gaze. 'Now that we've got that out of the way, perhaps you could give me a rundown of your duties?'

'I will... Only...'

'What?'

'I'm worried that because you're clearly angry with me about Tia you might deliberately find something wrong about the way I do my job so—so that you can get back at me in some way.'

'What?' Stunned, Dante widened his blue-grey eyes. 'Do you really think I'd resort to the kind of tactics that would jeopardise my daughter's well-being? Think about it. If I tried to punish you in some way, would it not have repercussions for her too? I'd hardly allow that.'

'You see? That's where our sticking point is. I don't know you well enough to know *what* you might be capable of.' Her slender shoulders lifted in a shrug. 'All I know is that it's been a confusing and worrying time, what with the threat of Anita and Grant possibly having to sell up and leave, and then—and then out of the blue you show up, and I learn that you're the man who's looking to invest in the hotel and will become the new senior partner. More importantly, I then have to break the news to you that Tia is your daughter. I had no idea how you'd react. We only spent a night together. You might feel utterly compromised and furious. Or you might…' Her voice faltered a little. 'You might want to try and take her away from me. Can you wonder why I couldn't sleep last night?'

Dante pushed to his feet, because the restlessness and annoyance that deluged him wouldn't allow him to remain sitting.

'Why would I want to try and take her away from you? Don't you think—to use an English expression— that would be rather like shooting myself in the foot? I can see that she adores you, and you her. From what I've seen you've done an admirable job of raising her by yourself. But I'm sticking by my original conviction that she needs her father in her life too. She needs two parents…which is why I said we should marry.'

'Why would you want to tie yourself to a woman you knew for just one night?' Anna's voice was slightly husky as she asked this, and a tiny perplexed crease puckered her brow.

'Because that one night resulted in a child…a child I didn't even know about until yesterday!' He drove his hands into his trouser pockets as he moved away from the desk, briefly presenting her with his back.

Was the impression he'd left her with so poor that she hadn't considered even for a moment trying to contact him? It didn't make Dante feel very good *or* wanted. It just made him mad. Briefly thinking of his father and his ex, he wondered what *rare* quality he had that made it so easy for people to walk away from him. And to make them think he wouldn't be concerned about his own flesh and blood.

'Dante?'

Garnering his composure, he turned back to face the striking redhead on the other side of the desk.

'What is it?'

'I didn't tell you before because I didn't quite know how to put it, but I *did* initially try to contact you when I found out I was pregnant. I did find out your name, and I even looked you up on the internet.'

'And?' Dante interjected impatiently, his heart thudding.

'Your reputation was quite—quite intimidating. To be perfectly honest, it worried me. I didn't even know if you'd remember me, let alone believe me when I told you I was pregnant. Anyway…' Glancing away, Anna heaved a sigh. 'I decided perhaps it was best after all if I didn't contact you. But some months after Tia was born the conviction that you had a right to know about her took hold of me again. For days I followed every lead I could to try and track you down, but it was as though you'd disappeared. Of course now I realise that it was because you'd changed your name. I went back to believing that maybe it had never been on the cards that we should meet again. In any case, for all I knew you could have married and had children with someone else. And besides…that night we were together you did tell me it was a one-time-only thing and that I had to accept that…remember?'

Dante remembered. He sombrely reflected on how he'd regretted that over the years. There had been many lonely nights when he would have been thrilled to have Anna in his arms again. But, to be brutal, at the time all he could have offered her was sex. Not even companion-ship had been an option. Not after his mother's death. He'd been in too dark a place to take anyone there with him. But it still hit him hard that because of his ruth-less reputation Anna had been frightened of trying to make contact. And later, when she'd wanted to try and find him again, he had changed his name back to Dante Romano. He could no longer blame her for anything. Everything that had happened was *his* fault.

'We cannot turn back the clock. That is beyond even *my* power, ruthless reputation or no.' His lips twisted ruefully. 'What has happened in the past has happened, and all we can do now is face what's in front of us today. Besides…our personal issues probably shouldn't be dis-cussed in work time. We'll talk tonight, as previously agreed. Right now I have an interview to conduct.'

He sat down again, automatically switching his brain to work mode. He'd turned that ability into a fine art over the years whenever emotions had threatened to swamp him. The woman sitting opposite him was silent.

'Anna?'

For a moment she seemed troubled. But then the corners of her pretty mouth curved into a smile.

'You mean you're not going to call me Miss Bailey any more?' she teased.

The look on her face was somewhere between angel and imp, and Dante all but groaned—because it was as though someone had shot a flame-tipped arrow straight into his loins. A charged memory of her whispering softly into his ear and moving over his body, erotically sliding her mouth over his as her long hair, carrying its scent of oranges and patchouli, drifted against him surfaced powerfully.

'When we're working together, and in the company of our colleagues, I may from time to time call you Miss Bailey. When we're alone…' his voice lowered meaningfully '…I'll call you Anna.'

'Right.' Beneath her flawlessly satin skin, a soft pink bloomed like a summer rose.

Gratified that he still had the power to discomfit her, Dante couldn't help the smile that escaped him.

'We'll carry on then…yes?'

'Yes, all right.' She straightened her back, but her expression seemed transfixed and he had to prompt her again.

'Anna?'

She patted down her hair.

'Sorry. To answer your question—my first responsibility is to the manager…to help support him in fulfilling the hotel's promise of delivering an impeccable service to the customer.'

'And how do you and Mr Cathcart get on? Do you communicate well? Are there any problems there, for instance?'

'There aren't any problems. Jason—Mr Cathcart and I have always got on. He's kind and fair…just like his parents.'

'So you like him?'

'Yes, I like him. We work very well together.'

'Good…that's good to hear.'

Twirling his pen absently between his fingers, now it was Dante's turn to fall into a trance. Studying the arresting face before him, the face that had haunted his sleep many nights in the past, he had a hungry need to just look and appreciate. To his mind, Anna Bailey's features were perfect. The finely shaped brows above those dancing long-lashed brown eyes, the slim and elegant nose and the pensive pretty mouth—there was a serenity about her that was more than a little appealing to a man who had lived his life mostly in the fast lane.

Did Jason Cathcart enjoy that aspect of her company too? He had certainly been voluble in his praise of Anna's talents and abilities during his interview with Dante earlier. A fierce little knot of jealousy throbbed painfully under his ribs. Did the man wish they were more than colleagues? he wondered. A disturbing image of him getting cosy with Anna and Tia almost stole his breath.

'And is Mr Cathcart good at leading and inspiring his staff, would you say?' he asked, gravel-voiced.

'Definitely.' A flicker of apprehension crossed Anna's face. 'You interviewed him earlier. Surely you formed an impression of him?'

'I did,' Dante answered abruptly. 'And that, of course, will remain confidential. Now, what other responsibilities does your role entail?'

Even though he would have preferred to quiz Anna further about *her* impression of her colleague, he knew it shouldn't be in the arena of a professional conversation concerning her job. Corralling the urge to ask her outright if she had more personal feelings towards Jason, he listened intently as she described other aspects of her role as assistant manager, determinedly making himself focus on the interview at hand and not get sidetracked by emotion.

CHAPTER SIX

THE ring on the doorbell just after she'd checked to see if Tia was asleep made Anna's heart skip a beat. She knew it was Dante. He had vowed he'd return later, after going back to his apartment. They'd agreed he would drop by after she'd put Tia to bed so that they could talk in private.

Glancing at the two slim-stemmed wine glasses she'd left on the coffee table, she nervously smoothed down the multicoloured jersey tunic dress that she'd hastily donned over black leggings and cinched with a vivid green belt, praying she didn't look as flustered as she felt.

'Hi.'

She hadn't known how starved she was for the sight of his sculpted, strikingly good-looking face until she was confronted by it at the door. Her pulse went wild. In turn, Dante's disturbing gaze ran up and down her figure with equally hard-to-hide intensity, and every flicker of his glance was like lighted touchpaper to already simmering embers.

'Come in,' she invited, her voice hoarse, practically pressing herself into the wall to let him pass.

'Nice perfume,' he remarked, low-voiced, as he entered, his eyes reflecting electric blue sparks tonight, rather than the dramatic hue of stormy seas. 'Sexy.'

'Thanks,' Anna murmured, her mind going unhelpfully blank at the compliment.

'I've brought some very good Italian wine.' He placed a dark slim bottle into her hands. 'It's a Barolo. It comes from a region known as Piedmont, where they're famed for making the best wines.'

'That's kind. I've got some dry white chilling in the fridge, but if you prefer red then that's fine with me. We can have either.' Shrugging self-consciously, she shut the door behind them, adding, 'I don't mind.'

Wishing she didn't feel as if she'd been shaken hard, then stood on her head, Anna led the way into the living room.

'When we first met, I didn't know you were Italian,' she remarked lightly.

'Only on my mother's side.'

'What about your father?'

'He was British.'

'That explains why you used the surname Masterson, then. You don't have much of an Italian accent, either.'

'I stopped residing in Italy a long time ago.'

'Why? Did your parents move to the UK?'

His fascinating eyes darkened almost warningly. 'No.

They didn't. They parted company when I was very young…younger than Tia, in fact.'

'And you didn't want to stay in Italy?'

'Enough questions for now, I think.'

There was a definite tightening to Dante's perfectly symmetrical jaw, and Anna clamped her teeth down on her lip, embarrassed at the flow of curiosity that had unstoppably rushed out. But frustration niggled her—because how were she and her daughter supposed to get to know him if he was so reluctant to reveal himself?

'Why don't you sit down?' she suggested, awkward now.

Dropping down onto the couch, his expression relieved, Dante undid the single button on his tailored black jacket to reveal a midnight-blue cashmere sweater. The golden lights in his hair glinted fiercely beneath the soft glow of one of the nearby lamps, the odd silver strand here or there making him look mouthwateringly distinguished. As if she wasn't already provocatively aware of his charismatic presence, the exotically eastern tones of his aftershave sensuously made a beeline into Anna's solar plexus and caused a near meltdown.

'Open the Barolo,' he said casually, gesturing towards the bottle in her hands. 'It's a cold, rainy night outside and it will warm us up.'

His barely perceptible smile pierced her heart. Why did it seem so hard for him to relax? What was it about his past that still racked him with shadows? she mused.

'Okay...I will.'

Briefly disappearing into the kitchen to locate the corkscrew, Anna was grateful for a few moments to herself. It was clear that the inflammatory attraction that had flared out of control that night five years ago had not dimmed one *iota*. At least not for *her*. To be frank, the realisation filled her with trepidation. How could she be clear-headed and wise and do the right thing for her and Tia if all Dante had to do was walk into a room to have her temperature shooting off the scale?

In the living room once more, she gladly gave the task of pouring the wine to him. Right then her hands weren't anywhere near steady enough to do it without the possibility of spilling some. As she crossed the room to the single plump armchair, Anna felt Dante's glance track her progress.

Before raising his glass to his lips, he asked, 'Is the baby asleep?'

Charmed and taken aback that he should refer to Tia as 'the baby' with such affection in his voice, she knew her smile was unreserved. 'Yes, she is.'

'I'd like to look in on her before I go tonight.'

'Of course.'

'There's so much about her I want to know... What food she likes, her favourite colour, the book she likes the most.'

His gaze seemed to take him away to distant shores for a moment, and Anna caught her breath as a merciless stab of guilt assailed her.

But before she could comment he continued, 'We should have a toast. To Tia and her happy future.'

'Tia and her happy future,' she concurred a little huskily, her mouth drying, because she knew that the future was one of the most pertinent things they had to discuss tonight. What would it entail? Not just for her precious child, but for Anna herself now that Dante had reappeared?

Sipping at her wine, she allowed the alcohol to swim warmly into her blood for a moment, hoping it might relax her. 'This is nice…it reminds me of violets somehow.'

'You have a good nose. Barolo *does* have a bouquet of violets. You could have a new career in wine-tasting.'

'Will I need a new career?'

'Your interview wasn't *that* bad.'

'How comforting,' she quipped, unable to hide the surge of annoyance that surfaced. 'I've had no complaints about how I carry out my job so far.'

'There's no need to be defensive. You've nothing to fear from me, Anna. I certainly don't have any plans to fire you from your job.'

To her alarm, Dante set his wine glass down on the coffee table and got to his feet. Then he was standing in front of her, his nearness making her feel quite light-headed.

'Put your wine down for a minute,' he commanded quietly, voice low.

Captured by his hypnotic glance, Anna obeyed. He held out his hand and helped her to her feet.

'That dress you're wearing hurts my eyes.'

Embarrassment made her want the floor to open up and swallow her.

'I know it's a bit dazzling, but I grabbed the first thing out of my wardrobe, to tell you the truth.' She was fumbling for a foothold but couldn't find one. Had his shoulders always been this wide...his chest this broad and strong? The male heat he emanated so—so *drugging*?

'It's dazzling not because of the riot of colour but because it's on *you*. Dazzling like this glorious hair of yours.' Capturing a handful of burnished copper silk between his fingers, Dante raised the fiery strands to his lips and kissed them.

Anna couldn't move. It took every ounce of iron will she possessed not to give in to the overwhelming impulse to lay her head against his chest and wrap her arms round his waist. The intoxication of his presence almost made her forget why he was there...*almost*.

'I am so glad you haven't had it cut short since I saw you last.'

'I—I wouldn't do that... But, Dante—we—we need to talk,' she murmured, her own voice sounding like a dazed stranger's.

'We can talk like we talked when we first met. Like this... Do you remember, Anna?'

The heat of his lips touched the side of her neck,

searing the delicate skin there with an indelible brand. 'I remember,' she husked, her limbs turning to liquid silver. 'But we should— We need to…' A helpless little moan escaped her as Dante moved his lips up to her ear, his mouth planting a hot, devastatingly erotic kiss on her highly sensitive lobe. The molten heat that pooled in Anna's centre threatened to make her lose her capacity to think at all.

'What do we need to do?'

With a smile in his voice that was a seductive cocktail of fine malt whisky and luxurious honey, Dante settled his hands on her hips and firmly pulled her against him. The hard male contours encased in his fluidly elegant tailored suit and the suggestion of barely con-tained impressive masculine strength made Anna shiver. Mesmerised by the haze of longing in his burning gaze, she nervously swallowed. She yearned to succumb to the desire that was flowing with equal ardour through her veins, but an anguished moment of clarity returned, making her stiffen in his arms.

'What did you mean when you said you weren't going to fire me from my job? I don't like the sound of that… It makes me feel like you potentially *could* fire me if you wanted to. I can't say that fills me with confidence… not when I have a child to support, and depend on my job for a roof over our heads.'

There was a flash of impatience in his eyes.

'The point is that you don't need to depend on your job to sustain you, *or* for a roof over your heads! I meant it when I said we should marry. And when we're married I'll take care of you both.'

'You make it sound so straightforward and easy. I'm not an investment you're interested in, Dante. I'm a fully functioning independent human being with my own ideas and thoughts on lots of subjects—including marriage. It's completely wrong of you to assume that I'd instantly give up everything I've worked so hard for to throw in my lot with a man I barely know. A man who only wants marriage because he's discovered that the one-night stand that we had resulted in a child!'

He set Anna free with a muttered oath and stalked across the room, scraping his fingers through the dark blond strands of his previously groomed hair. His glare was blistering in its intensity. 'What better reason to marry someone than because you made a child together? Tia deserves to have her father in her life. I want that for her and I want that for me—and as a "fully functioning independent human being" you have no right to deny us!'

'I'm not saying I'd deny you. But marriage isn't for me. I...' She lowered her gaze to stare down at the floor, 'I like my independence... I like the fact that my hard work has finally got me somewhere and now I have opportunities... I'm captain of my own ship and it's a good feeling.'

'So you like being captain of your own ship—but do you honestly like being alone? Raising a child on your own is far from easy, no matter how many opportunities for advancing your career come your way. When the baby is ill do you welcome being her sole carer, with no one but yourself to rely upon to make the best decisions for her welfare? And when she's ill what do you do if you can't take time off work for fear of losing your job and your income?'

Moving back across the room towards her, Dante had that faraway look Anna had seen before in his eyes.

'Once when I was five I had the measles...had it quite severely. My mother had no choice but to go out to her job in the evening—it was literally a matter of whether we ate or starved. She asked a close neighbour if I could stay with her for the evening, but the woman refused because she had five children of her own and didn't want to risk them getting infected. My mother left me in bed. The neighbour promised to regularly check up on me while she was gone. I had a raging fever, and by the time my mother came home I was convulsing. We didn't have a telephone. She ran with me through the night to a man she knew who owned a restaurant, and he called a doctor. If it weren't for that I probably wouldn't have made it.'

His tone bitterly rueful, he shook his head. 'My mother went to hell and back that night. If she had had someone to help her, someone who cared equally for my welfare, she wouldn't have suffered the torment and guilt that she did. And I have no intention of ever letting my daughter be in the precarious position I was...no matter what your assurances.'

Barely knowing how to answer him, Anna wept inside for the agony Dante and his mother must have endured that terrible night. It was the kind of nightmare scenario every mother dreaded.

Before she realised it her impulse to touch him, to comfort him in some way, overtook her, and she laid her hand against the side of his face. His skin was velvety warm, pulsing with the vibrant strength she'd detected earlier. 'I love that you care for Tia so deeply already. But I'm lucky, Dante... I may be a single mum, but I have friends—people who really care for Tia—people who would help us at the drop of a hat.'

'That may be so, but I have no intention of leaving my child's well-being to the precarious fair-weather attention of mere friends! No matter how much you might trust them, Anna. So...' He winced a little when she withdrew her hand, almost as if she'd struck him. 'There's only one solution to our dilemma, and I've already told you what that is. Now it's just a matter of arranging things. The sooner the better, I think.'

Stroking her hands up and down her arms, Anna sensed their tremble.

'I'm not getting married...I told you.'

'Then regrettably, you're pushing me into taking action I'd much rather not take,' Dante retorted. 'But I will take it if it means I can be with my daughter. I'll go to court to get full custody of Tia.'

Was it only to her own hypersensitive hearing that her heartbeat sounded so deafeningly loud? Anna thought.

She'd been musing on a mother's worst nightmare but surely this was one of the most horrendous threats a woman could face? That her child's estranged parent might sue for custody and take her away—maybe to live in another country entirely? Searching for compassion in Dante's flint-like stare, worryingly, she found none.

'No!' she protested loudly, tears stinging the backs of her lids.

He lifted an eyebrow, but looked no less resolved on his course. 'If you don't want me to take such an action, then I suggest you stop putting obstacles in the way and agree to our marriage.'

'That's so disrespectful. You'd resort to something as low as blackmail to get your own way?'

'I told you.' His broad-shouldered shrug was unapologetic. 'I'll do anything I can to be with my daughter… the daughter you have so callously denied me knowledge of for four years because my so-called reputation made you believe I didn't deserve to know about her. And you have the audacity to stand there and lecture *me* on respect!'

'I didn't keep her from you deliberately.' Wanting to cry in frustration as well as pain, Anna stared pleadingly into the heartbreakingly handsome features of the well-dressed man in front of her. 'Don't you think I would have preferred to be in a good relationship with my baby's father than be asked not to try and get in touch after we parted that night? I know it was a difficult time for you, but it didn't exactly make me feel wanted to know that you could just walk away from me and never look back. And how do you think I felt when I discovered I was pregnant? Especially when it was the first time I—' She bit her lip on what she'd been going to say and continued, 'I was shocked, lonely, scared... I experienced every one of those states—but even taken together they don't come near to describing how I felt.'

She noticed that Dante's glance was quizzical.

'It was the first time you...what, Anna?'

Backing up nervously, she reached for the glass of wine she'd left on the side-table near the armchair and drank some. She let the alcohol hit before raising her chin with a defiant air born of Dutch courage. Her dark eyes focused firmly on Dante.

'It was the first time I'd slept with a man.'

The oath he swore was in Italian, and because she was shaky after revealing her news Anna returned her glass to the table, waiting for the tirade of disbelief that she was certain would explode towards her.

But when next he spoke Dante's voice was surprisingly quiet, his words measured. 'You were untouched when I took you into my bed...that's what you're telling me?'

'I was. Couldn't you tell I was no experienced seductress who made a habit of going to bed with male guests? I'd barely even been kissed before!'

'Yet you were molten heat in my arms. Everywhere I touched you, you made me burn.'

Praying for some way to steady the deluge of emotion that tumbled forcefully through her, Anna despaired of ever feeling calm again when she saw the renewed flame of Dante's desire sinfully reflected back at her...just as if it had never gone away. With a disparaging toss of her head, she answered, 'I think I lost my mind a little that night. I would never usually behave in that way with a strange man...with *any* man for that matter.'

'We lost our minds together, Anna.' He sounded seductively accepting and non-judgmental. 'And the result was little Tia. Can you regret such an outcome?'

'Never.'

'Then we have to deal with this situation like adults, instead of feuding children, and that means our daughter's welfare takes priority.'

'You mean...' Anna surveyed him with a frown. 'You mean you still believe marriage is the only answer?'

'I do.'

'If that's the way you want to go, how about trying a trial period of living together first?'

'Too uncertain—and it hardly represents the security I want for Tia.'

'Surely that depends on how we deal with it? If we're committed to making it work, then living together could be just as secure as marriage.'

'No. That's not what I want.'

'And if I refuse? You'd really take me to court for custody?'

'I would.' His piercing glance was as unyielding as ice.

CHAPTER SEVEN

It DIDN'T exactly enhance his self-esteem or his pride, having to potentially resort to blackmail to persuade Anna to marry him, but since he had made the earth-shattering discovery that he was a father, Dante's determination to help bring up his daughter was cast-iron. There was nothing the redheaded beauty could say that would deter him.

But in truth he was taken aback that she could so easily refuse him. He'd met plenty of women on his travels who considered him quite the catch.

Once upon a time his ex-wife Marisa had said those very words to him. *'You're quite a catch, Dante... It's a wonder that you've been allowed to say free and single for this long...'*

But that assertion by her had soon turned to ashes when she'd discovered that for her husband raw ambition came first and his most intimate relationship a very poor second. Even when his marriage had been in its dying stages he hadn't sought to rescue it, or been able to express his emotions. Marisa had walked into the arms of another man and Dante had simply let her—if he was honest, feeling nothing but relief.

Now the greatest shock that he had ever received...the news that he was a *father*...reverberated doubly on learning that Anna had been a sexual innocent when he'd slept with her. It also made him remember the flicker of apprehension in her eyes when, for a few moments as she lay beneath him, he'd sensed definite tension in her slender frame. What must she have thought when he'd asked her to spend the night and then warned her not to expect anything else? Not a phone call, not even his real name—nothing! What an introduction to the world of adult relationships she'd had.

Fast forward five years on, and Dante knew that if he'd met Anna today he would never have let her go... not for all the million-dollar real estate in the world. With her gorgeous flame hair flowing unhindered over her shoulders and her brown eyes sparkling like fire-warmed brandy she was vivacious, pretty and completely unpretentious. Her eye-catching dress with its patent green belt highlighted how tiny her waist was, and the black leggings she wore cleaved lovingly to her long, model-slim legs.

Studying her now, he acknowledged that she made the blood pound through his veins like no other woman he'd ever met. So, even if she despised him for putting her in such a compromising position, he would endeavour not to disappoint her as he had disappointed his ex. He certainly wouldn't give her cause to accuse him of ignoring her. He would also show her that he intended to be the best father to Tia that a child could have. She would not want for anything materially, and for as long as he lived Dante would dote on her. There would be no need for Anna to be lonely either, because he fully intended to keep her warm at nights and reintroduce her to the delight and pleasure of passionate lovemaking...

Having returned to the old-fashioned floral armchair, she now sat nursing her wine glass, her glance wary and resentful when it locked with his.

'I'll have to tell the Cathcarts about us,' she murmured.

'Yes, you will.' Shrugging off his jacket, Dante dropped it onto the arm of the couch. Turning back to Anna, he smiled enigmatically. 'But don't worry... they'll have plenty of time to absorb the news.'

'Why's that?'

'Because after discussing the changes that need to be implemented I'm going to suggest we close the hotel for a month while it's being refurbished and modernised. In that time we will travel to Lake Como with Tia, where you and I will marry.'

'You're intending to close the Mirabelle for a whole month?' Slamming her wine glass precariously on the side-table, Anna widened her brown eyes in disbelief. 'What about the staff? What about their jobs? They can't possibly afford to take a whole month off.'

'It will be paid leave.' An irritated muscle flinched hard in the side of Dante's cheekbone. He'd just told her he was taking her to Lake Como to marry him and all she could think about was what was going to happen to the staff! It seriously irked him that Anna's soft heart did not include fretting about *him* in such a concerned manner.

'Can you afford to do that?' she asked in wonder.

He could have replied that he could buy and refurbish the hotel and fund the staff's leave several hundred times over and still have change, but Dante didn't. The stunning house he owned in Lake Como would be a surprise and hopefully a delight to her when she saw it, and perhaps would bring home to her just how wealthy her soon-to-be husband actually was. But there was a hollow feeling in the pit of his stomach that he should take refuge in something so superficial when in truth he wanted Anna to regard him totally for himself, to see the man behind the thousand dollar suits and impressive portfolio, *not* what his money could buy.

'I have interests in several very successful businesses worldwide, Anna, so trust me...' His hand cut expressively through the air. 'Worrying about whether I can afford it is not something that even has to enter your head.'

She was puzzled that he seemed so annoyed. Had she dented his ego by querying whether he could afford to do as he'd said? But, more perturbing than that, Anna was under siege from far more unsettling concerns. Events were moving at a pace she hadn't remotely expected, and one major issue was disturbing her above all else.

Dante's insistence that they marry was making her feel as though he wanted to control and possess her, and was disturbingly reminiscent of her father's behaviour as she was growing up.

Frank Bailey had had two major passions in his life… his love affair with booze and his diminutive, too passive wife—Anna's mother, Denise. He'd been so possessive and jealous that he'd completely banned her from even having friends, because he couldn't bear her attention to be on anyone else but him. That jealousy had even transferred itself to Anna if he thought she was too demanding—which even as a small child she rarely was. But her father had been able to misread the most innocent situations, and had made his judgements with an authority that chilled the blood.

Consequently, Anna had lost count of the times she'd witnessed his rage—and that included being frequently belittled by him verbally. An occurrence that had become even more frightening and threatening to her peace of mind when he was drunk. She knew intimately that mental torment was just as destructive as physical violence. There were too many times when, upon hearing her father's key in the door, she'd sat on her bed quaking with terror, praying to disappear, praying for a greater power to make her so small that he wouldn't even notice she was there.

In agitation, she rose to her feet. 'Dante…about us going to Lake Como to—to get married…'

'What about it?'

She obviously *had* upset him, because his handsome face was fierce for a moment. But, however unapproachable he seemed, Anna refused to be intimidated by him.

'I'll go with you on one condition.'

'I have already told you that—'

'Hear me out.' Although shaking inside, her tone was unerringly firm, and there was a definite flash of surprise in Dante's light-coloured eyes. 'I don't want a wedding arranged until I see how we get on together. And I won't have you issuing me with threats of going to court for custody of Tia either. I've seen the damage it can do to a woman's spirit to have a man try to control her, and I won't accept it from anyone...not even and *especially* the man who fathered my child!'

'You're speaking from personal experience?' Although Dante's voice had turned quiet, it was underscored with shock and a sense of impatience too—as if he wanted to hear the full extent of what Anna had endured.

'Yes, I am.' She crossed her arms in front of her, knowing there was no point in keeping her past a secret. It wouldn't serve her in the long run, however painful it was to talk about it. Ghosts could only haunt a person if they colluded with them to keep them hidden. 'My father was a cruel and jealous drunk, and he made my mother's life a living hell.'

'Where is he now?'

'No longer in this world…thank goodness.' An icy shudder ran down Anna's spine.

'And your mother…where is she?'

'She's gone too.' She briefly pursed her lips, fighting hard to win the struggle over her tears. 'They said at the hospital that she died of heart disease, but I know that's not what killed her. She was simply tired and worn out… beaten down by living with my brute of a father.'

His glance glinting with anger as well as sympathy, Dante stepped towards her. 'Was he a brute to you too, Anna?' he demanded huskily.

'A man with a propensity for intimidation doesn't care who he tries to intimidate. He just gets off on the power. His children are the easiest targets of all—especially when they're too scared to answer back in case they get another verbal lashing. And the situation becomes even more horrendous when the impulse to dominate and show what a big strong man he is is fuelled by alcohol.'

Shame and despair cramped her throat for a second. 'Have you any idea what it's like to have foul beer or whisky-smelling breath right in your face, and a mocking voice yelling at you how useless you are? How worthless? Anyway, I don't want to talk any more about this right now.' She made as if to move towards the kitchen. 'I don't think I can drink any more wine, lovely as it is. I think I'll make some coffee. Would you like some?'

'No.' Dante laid his hand on her arm to prevent her from turning away, but he didn't curl his fingers to grip it. Right now he needed to tread very carefully. He could see the fear and terror in her eyes from her disturbing memories and it shook him deeply. 'We'll do as you suggest. We'll go to Lake Como and live together for a while before embarking on marriage. Does that make you happier, Anna?'

Perversely, the look of relief crossing her face was like a hammer blow to Dante. He didn't want to possess Anna—he knew that would be wrong. In the light of what she'd experienced with her bullying father it would be *doubly* wrong. Just the thought of such a man hurting her in any way brought out the most base of animal instincts in him to deal with *anyone* who threatened her or Tia. Ultimately all he wanted to do was take care of them both—to show Anna that beneath the facade of wealth and success his genuine heartfelt desire was for family and connection. He wanted the chance to prove that underneath the outward material trappings and his drive for achievement existed the good, responsible, caring man that his mother had always insisted was the *real* Dante Romano.

'Thank you,' she answered softly.

Reluctantly he let go of her arm, even though touching her through the material of her dress made him long for so much more.

'Perhaps while you make your coffee I could look in on Tia? I just want to sit beside her bed and watch her sleep for a while,' he said.

'Go ahead. Take as long as you like.'

* * *

Half an hour later, Anna opened Tia's bedroom door to find Dante comfortably ensconced in the cosy slipper chair beside their daughter's bed, his elbows resting against his long-boned thighs in his exquisitely tailored suit trousers and his body quite still. His avid gaze was transfixed by the angelic blond child who lay sleeping peacefully beneath the Walt Disney character–decorated pink duvet, one arm flung out by her side and the other clutching her favourite chewed teddy bear.

Anna needed a moment. It was as though one of her favourite made-up stories had come to startling, vivid life, and she hardly dared breathe for fear of disturbing it and making it disappear.

But Dante had heard her come in and, turning in his chair, treated her to the most disarming, knee-trembling smile she'd ever seen.

'She's so beautiful,' he breathed quietly. 'I don't want to leave her…not for a minute or even a second. I've missed so much of her growing up.'

Anna didn't mistake the catch in his voice. Advancing into the room, which was illuminated only by the soft night light glowing in the corner, she dropped her hand on his hard-muscled shoulder, silently thrilling to feel the sensuous warmth that emanated through the luxurious cashmere of his sweater.

'She's still got a lot of growing up to do, Dante…she's only four. And children quickly adapt to new situations and people. One day she'll forget there was even a time when you didn't mean the world to her.'

Covering her hand and holding it against him, Dante held Anna's gaze with a passionate heated look. 'I want her to know I'm her father. I want her to know as soon as possible. Can you understand that?'

Gripped by the pain in his voice, Anna breathed out slowly. 'I do. Of course I do. But we just—we just have to pick the right moment.'

'Tomorrow when you pick her up from school we'll take her somewhere for tea. It will give her and me the chance to get to know each other a little. But I don't want her to be kept in the dark about who I am for long, Anna.' He let go of her hand. 'I don't think I could bear that.'

'We'll tell her soon,' she said reassuringly, seeing by his expression how in earnest he was about Tia knowing he was her father.

Clenching his jaw for a moment, Dante exhaled a heavy sigh. His eyes flashed like distant lightning in a velvet midnight sky.

'Good...that's good. Now, I think it's probably time I left. We have much to do tomorrow. I'll see you in the morning, Anna.' His lips brushed briefly against her cheek as he stood up. 'Try to get some proper sleep tonight, eh?'

The sensuous trail of his cologne and the seductive warmth that was the legacy of his lips lingered on Anna's skin long after he had gone...

She asked if Anita could spare a few minutes to talk during their afternoon tea break. Expressing her usual amicable concern, the older woman kindly welcomed Anna into the office she shared with her husband—an entirely organised and *smart* office in comparison with her son Jason's. Grant had gone out to visit a new supplier and wouldn't be back until later, she confided.

She appeared much happier, Anna noticed—as if a world of worry had been lifted from her shoulders. Dante's rescue package for the Mirabelle was already making a difference, she realised. There was no doubt in her mind that he would turn the hotel's fortunes around. He was an accomplished, experienced investor, and even their sous chef Cheryl, and Amy and Linda the receptionists, were already referring to him as their 'knight in shining armour'. She didn't know why their praise and ingratiating admiration should put her back up, but it did.

'What's troubling you, sweetheart?' Stirring her tea, Anita sat back in one of the three easy chairs arranged round a coffee table, surveying Anna with concern.

'Am I that easy to read?' the younger woman quipped.

'Not always… But for some reason today I definitely sense that you're anxious about something.'

'It's about Dante,' Anna began, her fingers knotting together in her lap.

Her cheeks flamed red when Anita raised a curious eyebrow. The casual form of address had slipped out, because he'd been on her mind almost constantly since last night. Especially when she remembered that look on his face and the tremor in his voice when he'd passionately declared that he wanted Tia to know he was her father.

'I mean Mr Romano,' she corrected herself quickly.

'What's wrong? I know he's been a little…shall we say *abrasive* with you, dear—but he can be extraordinarily thoughtful of people too. He's already won friends here. And when he's talked to me and Grant about plans for updating the hotel he's consulted our opinion at every turn. There are exciting plans afoot!' Her lips splitting in a grin reminiscent of an excited schoolgirl, Anita all but hugged herself. 'We're going to call a staff meeting later, to give everyone an update, but as you're our assistant manager I may as well tell you confidentially that Dante has deemed it a good idea to close the Mirabelle for a month while the modernisation gets underway. All the staff will get paid leave.'

'How do you feel about that?'

'We're perfectly happy. Not only is it necessary, but it's a great idea too. Grant and I haven't had a break in so long. We plan to devote some time to our much neglected garden, and spend some genuine quality time together. You should think about having a little holiday, Anna…you work so hard and you and Tia deserve it.'

'Maybe I will.' Shrugging lightly, Anna wished she could hear herself think over the clamouring of her heart. 'Look, Anita…there's no way of couching this or making it sound less surprising…I've got something important to tell you.'

'You're not handing in your notice?'

'No.' Anna took a nervous swallow. 'It's something much more personal. You know I've never told you before who Tia's father is?'

Anita stared, her gaze intrigued. The ticking wall clock suddenly seemed noisily loud.

'Well, it's—'

'Yes?'

'It's Dante Romano.'

Beneath her carefully applied make-up, her boss paled a little in shock. 'Dante Romano? But how can that be? As far as I'm aware he's never been here before, so how could you two have met?'

'He *has* been here before.' Clearing her throat, Anna smiled awkwardly. 'It was about five years ago. I was working the late shift in the bar, and he—he was there having a drink. He'd just returned from Italy, where he'd been to his mother's funeral, and had stopped en route to New York, where he was living at the time.'

'And you and he…?'

Lifting her chin, because she wouldn't be ashamed of that incredible life-changing night, Anna met her boss's brown-eyed glance without flinching.

'There was an immediate attraction and we slept to-gether that was how I fell pregnant with Tia.'

CHAPTER EIGHT

'Anna, can I have a word?'

She was walking by Jason's office when he opened the door and beckoned to her. Having had their staff meeting, everyone was now perfectly aware of the imminent plan to close the hotel for a month while it was being modernised, but she hadn't had an opportunity to discuss it with the manager—especially the news that he'd been made project manager to oversee the refurbishments while everyone else was away. No doubt that was why he wanted to see her. It was a big step up for him, and a huge responsibility. But Anna had no doubts that Jason could do it.

Regarding her relationship with Dante, Anita Cathcart had suggested that they keep it to themselves for a while—at least until the changes were underway and the staff had returned from leave. It was cowardly, but Anna's relief that she wouldn't be the focus of curious speculation just yet was boundless.

Shutting the door behind them Jason invited Anna

to sit down. 'You look very nice,' he commented, his glance running lightly over her outfit.

'I'm collecting Tia, then we're going out to have tea.'

'Going anywhere special?'

'I'm not sure yet, but we'll find somewhere nice, I'm sure. We're spoiled for choice in Covent Garden, aren't we?'

Her heart was thudding a little at the idea of telling her little girl some time soon that Dante was her father, and her smile was uncertain. But Jason seemed preoccupied with own problems as he started to restlessly pace the floor.

When he stopped pacing to nervously return his attention to Anna his dark eyes were shining. 'I've met someone,' he said in a rush.

'You have?' He'd been single for a long time, and didn't have much confidence in blind dates or being hooked up by some well-meaning friend as a means of finding 'the one', so Anna was genuinely pleased for him.

'I won't say any more just yet, in case I jinx things, but we're seeing each other this weekend.'

'Oh, Jason, that's wonderful—and of course you won't jinx things!'

Getting to her feet, she threw her arms round him in an affectionate hug.

Someone rapped on the door and stepped into the room before Jason could invite them. *It was Dante.* Anna had no reason in the world to feel guilty, but when his frosted gaze alighted on them, radiating obvious disapproval, she felt awkward and embarrassed—like a child caught red-handed, raiding the fridge after bedtime.

'I've been looking for Anna,' he said to Jason without preamble. 'A staff member suggested I see if she was with you. Looks like I hit the jackpot.'

'We were—we were just talking.' Flashing him an uncomfortable smile, Jason stepped quickly away from the girl at his side.

'Well, if you've finished *talking*, Anna and I have to go. We have some important business to attend to.'

'Isn't she taking her daughter out to tea?' The younger man's brow was furrowing.

'I see that you like to keep completely up to date with Miss Bailey's diary, Mr Cathcart. It would be nice if you could be as diligent in looking over that list of new equipment for the hotel that I left you, and let me have your thoughts first thing in the morning. This is an absolutely vital responsibility you've accepted, becoming project manager, and the work begins right here, right now. Don't let me down.' Holding the door open for Anna, Dante was impatient. 'We really have to go,' he said firmly.

'You didn't have to be so snooty or condescending to Jason. We've done nothing wrong.'

She had to practically run to keep up with Dante's annoyed stride as she followed him out into the hotel car park. Reaching a gleaming silver Jaguar, she heard an electronic key open the doors. He stopped dead, and she could see he was struggling with his temper.

'So you fling your arms round every male you work with, do you?'

'That's ridiculous. Of course I don't! He'd just told me some good news and I was pleased for him…that's all.'

The resentment in Dante's mercurial eyes receded only slightly.

'He likes you,' he said flatly.

Was he jealous? Anna let the thought swirl around for a bit, then mentally filed it to look at later. But she couldn't help her lips curving into a smile.

'And I like *him*. But not in the way you're insinuating.'

He would have liked to have quizzed her more, she saw, but instead he glanced down at the linked gold watch glinting on his wrist beneath his cuff and opened the passenger door for her.

'We'd better get going if we're not going to be late collecting Tia.'

'Where are we going for tea?' she asked lightly, before climbing into her seat.

'The Ritz Hotel.'

Dismay washed over her.

'You might have told me that earlier… I would have worn something smarter than this dress.'

It was a plain white linen dress that she'd teamed with

a businesslike black jacket, and the ensemble had had many outings in the past. It was perfect for a mild spring day like today, when there was just a gentle breeze blowing, but, knowing where they were heading, she was suddenly seized by the idea that it was nowhere near presentable enough for such a notoriously swish hotel.

His appreciative glance on the slender length of leg she unwittingly flashed as she sat down in her seat in a huff, Dante grinned and disarmed her completely.

'There is nothing wrong with what you are wearing, so there's no need to fret...*le guarda piu di bene a caro prezzo.*'

'And that means?'

'It means that you look more than fine.'

Dipping his head to survey Anna before closing her door, he let his light-filled gaze linger teasingly on her lips for a moment. Then it intensified. Suddenly there didn't seem to be enough air for her to breathe.

'Let's go and collect our little one, shall we?' Closing the passenger door, he moved with his usual fluid graceful stride round the Jaguar's bonnet to the driver's seat.

Tia wanted another scone and jam, and with Anna's agreement Dante leaned forward to spread the strawberry jam for her. *He'd never felt so proud.* Not one of his achievements had elicited the euphoria that poured through him now, when he surveyed this beautiful golden-haired child and knew he'd played an important part in her being.

Moving his glance across to Anna, he discovered her sherry-brown eyes were furtively studying him. With her river of auburn hair spilling unfettered down her back, and her quiet understated beauty, it was inevitable that she drew many admiring glances from the other guests taking afternoon tea. Mentally, Dante puffed out his chest. She was the mother of his child, and one day soon...*very soon* if he had his way...she would be his wife too. Yet, because of what she'd revealed about her cruel and controlling father, he needed to curb any inclination to manipulate her—even if waiting for her to say yes to marriage frustrated the hell out of him.

Her distressing childhood with such a despicable bully genuinely pained him. If Anna had been anything like their daughter, then she must have been the most exquisite, engaging little girl, and had surely deserved a man far more worthy to take care of her than the poor excuse for a father she'd had?

'This is a *golden* room,' Tia announced, licking strawberry jam off her lips as she chewed her second mouthwatering scone. 'There's a golden arch and golden tables and golden—what did you say those sparkly lamps on the ceiling were?'

'Chandeliers.'

'Yes—and golden chairs too! A king or a queen could live here. The people that own this place should call it the golden room—don't you think, Mummy?'

Reaching out to clean away some of the jam stains on her cherubic face with a linen napkin, Anna smiled. 'This is a very famous room, Tia, and it already has a name. It's called the Palm Court.'

'But,' Dante said softly, his voice lowering conspiratorially, 'from now on the three of us will always call it the golden room...deal?'

He held out his hand and Tia shook it enthusiastically, clearly delighted that the man who had brought them to such a magical place thought it was a good idea too.

'You have to shake Mummy's hand as well, Dante.'

'Of course...how silly of me to forget to do such an important thing.'

As soon as he took Anna's slim cool palm into his, the rest of the room faded away. The only thing Dante knew for sure was that his heart beat faster and heavier than it had before he'd touched her, and that if they had been alone he would have shown her in no uncertain terms that he desired her...*desired her beyond belief.* Immediately recognising the flare of heat suddenly laid bare in the liquid brown depths of her beautiful eyes, he inwardly rejoiced.

'You're meant to just shake her hand, not hold it for ages and ages!' his daughter protested huffily, pulling his hand away from her mother's with a distinctly old-fashioned look.

'Mind your manners, Tia, that was very rude.' Anna admonished her, looking embarrassed.

'I'm sorry.' The tips of the dark blond lashes that

were so like Dante's own briefly swept her cheeks in contrition, but a scant moment later her eyes shone with unrepentant mischief again. '*You're* not cross with me, are you?' She dimpled up at him.

That knock-out smile could melt his heart at a hundred paces, her father silently acknowledged. Tenderly he grazed his knuckles over her velvet cheekbone. 'No, *mia bambina*…I don't think I could be cross with you if I tried…you are far too charming and lovely for that.'

'She certainly has her moments.' Taking a sip of her Earl Grey tea in its exquisite porcelain cup, Anna replaced the delicate vessel back in its saucer before grimacing at Dante.

'Meaning?'

'Meaning that occasionally she can be a bit wild.'

'I wonder where she gets that from?' His tone was silky smooth and playful.

Surprising him with a grin, Anna tipped her head to the side.

'I can't imagine you ever doing anything that wasn't measured and considered, Dante. You just seem so organised and in charge to me—as if nothing life can throw at you could ever give you a moment's doubt about your place in the scheme of things.'

'You are wrong about that.' Feeling the need to put her right about her assumption, Dante was suddenly serious. 'Being part-Italian, passion is in my blood. Neither can I admit to never having a moment's doubt. Do you know a human being who can?'

'No,' she answered thoughtfully, 'I don't think I do.'

'What are you talking about, Mummy? It doesn't sound very interesting.'

Tia was clearly miffed at not being privy to the grown-ups' conversation. Turning her gaze to her daughter, Anna appeared to be thinking hard.

'Tia? There's something important I want to tell you.' Glancing over at Dante, she lowered her gaze meaningfully with his.

His heart pounded hard. He hadn't expected her to raise the subject on this outing, but now, realising that she was going to, he mentally began to arrange his armour—so that if Tia should protest the idea in any way the blow wouldn't wound him irreparably. Logically he knew it would take time for his daughter to learn to love him, but Dante craved her love and acceptance of him more than he could say.

'Mummy? I know you want to tell me something important, but I want to ask Dante something.' The child put her elbows on top of the white tablecloth and then, with her chin resting in her hand, studied him intently.

'What is it, sweetheart?'

'Are you married?'

Resisting the urge to laugh out loud at the uncanny aptness of the question, he endeavoured to keep his face expressionless so that Tia wouldn't think he wasn't giving her question the proper consideration.

'No, my sweet little girl...I'm not married.'

'My mummy's not married either. I wish she was. I wish she was so that I could have a daddy, like my friend Madison at school. Not all the children in my class have daddies, but she does, and I think she's very lucky—don't you?'

Powerful emotion struck Dante silent. As if in slow motion—as if time had ground to a dreamlike halt—he saw Anna's pale slim hand reach out to pull Tia's hand away from her chin and tenderly hold it.

'Darling, I want you to listen very carefully to what I need to tell you. Will you do that?'

Her blue-grey eyes widening like twin compact disks, Tia nodded gravely.

'Dante and I knew each other a long time ago—remember I told you that? Anyway, we liked each other very much. But unfortunately…because something very sad happened in Italy, where he came from…he had to go away.' Sighing softly, Anna gave him a brief heartfelt glance. 'When he left… When he left, I found out that I was expecting a baby.'

'A baby? That must have been me!'

'Yes, darling…it *was* you.'

Her innocent brow puckering, Tia swung her gaze round to alight firmly on Dante.

'Does that mean that you're my daddy, then?'

'Yes, my angel.' His throat feeling as if it had been branded with an iron, Dante attempted a smile. 'It does.'

'You mean my *real* daddy? Real like Madison's daddy is her *real* daddy?'

'Yes.'

'Then we must be a real *family*.'

Never had anyone looked clear down to his soul as his daughter did at that breathtaking moment, and he knew...*knew* beyond any shadow of doubt...that she saw him for who he really was. It was the most unsettling yet exhilarating feeling Dante had ever experienced.

'And if we're a real family then you have to come and live with us—because that's what real families do, you know. Mummy, can I have a chocolate éclair now?' Tia turned pleadingly towards her mother. 'If you don't want me to eat a whole one, in case I'm sick, can I share it with you and have just half?'

'Okay, but I think after that you should call it a day on the cake front, don't you?'

As Anna glanced at Dante with a tremulous smile, he silently formed the words *thank you*. Then, reaching towards the multi-tiered cake stand, he plucked a chocolate éclair from it and with the small silver knife by his plate proceeded to cut it in half...

It had been a day of truth-telling. Along with the relief that had followed it, an incredible fatigue rolled over Anna, dragging at her limbs and making her eyelids so heavy that she could hardly stay awake.

Having left Dante in the bedroom, watching Tia as

she drifted off to sleep after the story he'd read her, she kicked off her shoes and stretched out on the couch.

She'd told him that children quickly adapted to new situations and she'd been right. Already Tia was calling him Daddy—as if by voicing her acknowledgement of who he was gave her even more right to claim him as her own. It touched Anna almost unbearably to see father and child together, bonding as naturally as if there had never at any time been a separation. It was wonderful…a dream come true. *But where did that leave her?*

She'd been a single parent for so long. It wouldn't be easy to let go of that role, even when she knew it was probably best for Tia that her father was in her life at last. Was it wrong of her to feel so afraid? To live in fear that her autonomy over their lives would be taken away? And would it be wise to contemplate letting her loneliness be soothed by this rugged and virile urbane man to whom she'd relinquished her innocence one night five years ago, knowing that because of the wall she'd glimpsed behind his eyes more than once he'd probably never be able to love her the wholehearted way that he loved his daughter?

'How are you doing?'

Anna's eyes had been drifting closed, and suddenly Dante was there in front of her, staring down at her with his soulful light eyes in a way that would have made her knees knock together if she'd been standing.

'I'm fine, thanks. Just a bit tired, to tell you the truth.' She started to sit up, but he gestured that she stay just as she was and then dropped down to sit on the edge of the couch beside her.

The strong, long-fingered hands that she'd noticed when they first met and had privately thought poetic and artistic were linked loosely in front of him, and a lock of dark blond hair flopped sexily down in front of his forehead. His sculpted lean profile and long luxuriant lashes made him look like a movie star, and for a distressing moment Anna wondered what an outstanding male specimen like him could possibly see in someone as ordinary as her.

'It's been quite an incredible day, huh?'

And as Dante smiled at her with surprising warmth her suddenly wobbly self-esteem was completely banished beneath the breathtaking gaze that was directed straight at her…

CHAPTER NINE

'TIA loved the Ritz. She'll probably look round the Mirabelle now and think it quite shabby after being there.'

'That will be the last thing this hotel will be when we get through with all the improvements I have in mind. Did I tell you I've hired a team of designers from Milan to oversee the refurbishment?'

'Milan? Gosh.'

'This place is already in a league of its own as a Georgian building with a fascinating history. With modernisation and refurbishment it's going to be one of the most stylish and sophisticated establishments in London.'

'Anita and Grant deserve it to be. They've unstintingly lavished their love on it ever since Grant inherited it from his parents. Can I ask you something?'

He nodded.

'Talking about Milan…I was wondering…'

'Yes?'

'Does that mean you've made your peace with Italy?

It's just that you seemed reluctant to discuss it. You told me you left a long time ago, and I sensed that you had deliberately distanced yourself from it.'

'I had… But when I went back for my mother's funeral I remembered things about the place that I loved and missed. Gradually over the years I've grown to love it again. That's why I bought a house there…the house we will stay in when you and Tia return with me. Does that reply satisfy your question?'

Touching the tips of his fingers to her cheek, Dante studied her intently. Anna fell silent, hardly knowing what to say. He'd admitted that he'd distanced himself from his homeland but he hadn't said *why*. Would he ever trust her enough to disclose some of the secrets from his past? she wondered. But Lake Como was the other subject she needed to address.

'It's a big step for me to go with you to Italy. To tell you the truth, I feel a little vulnerable going there with you, Dante. I don't know the language, and I know you won't like this but I'm also wary of being pushed into something I'm not really ready for. Do you understand that?'

'It is not my intention to push you into anything or to make you feel vulnerable,' he replied thoughtfully. 'I simply want us to have a holiday together, for us to get to know one another and for Tia to get to know me. When you are ready, and *only* when you are ready, will we talk about marriage.'

'Do you mean it?'

He studied her gravely. 'My word is my bond.'

'I suppose I could do with a holiday. And, like you say…it will give you and Tia a chance to get to know each other a bit more.'

'And as for not speaking the language…I will make it my personal mission to teach you,' Dante promised. 'I will have you speaking like a native Italian before you know it! Tia too.'

'It's getting dark.' Nervously Anna glanced up at the swiftly fading evening light, evident through the room's high windows. At the same time she heard the lilting song of a lone blackbird. For some reason it made her feel a little melancholy. 'I ought to turn on the lamps.'

'Don't.' The command in Dante's tone gave her a jolt.

'It's gloomy…I'd like some light in here.'

'You're uncomfortable with the dark? There's no need when I am right here beside you, Anna. I would never let anything or anyone hurt you.'

His heated glance was in earnest, she saw. Instantly a swarm of butterflies fluttered wildly inside her.

'Yes, but I still want to… I still need some…some light.'

As she made to move, Dante slid his hand round to the back of her head, to bring her face slowly but inexorably towards his. The last thing she registered was his hot, languorous gaze before his mouth fell on hers to ravish it without restraint, his warm velvet tongue gliding and coiling sensually with hers, his breathing a grated rasp as the shadow of his beard scraped her chin.

A sea of honey lapped inside Anna. It was as though she'd been left languishing in a cold dark cave for five long years and now at last she was wildly, deliriously free again—free to breathe in pure heady oxygen and be deluged in light. The pleasure and joy that soared inside her was untrammelled as her hands pushed through the silky strands of Dante's fair hair to anchor his head as he anchored hers, all the better for their lips to meld and sup as though their hunger would never be assuaged. *Not in this lifetime...*

'No... Not—not here.' She gulped down a shaky breath as his hands tugged at the zip fastener on her dress. 'My bedroom.'

They didn't let each other go as they entered the dim, cool enclave of Anna's room. It seemed essential to keep touching, to keep holding on in case some nightmare schism should cut through their longing and keep them apart for ever.

With the heel of his Italian loafer Dante shut the door behind them. He shucked off his footwear just before falling onto the bed with her, somehow manoeuvring her on top of him as he kissed her senseless. The zipper on her linen dress was skilfully undone, the sleeves tugged urgently down over her shoulders. With dreamlike effort Anna helped Dante remove it completely, then she was astride his hard lean hips again, bending her head to give and receive drugging, passionate kisses that made her head spin and her heart gallop. Her long waving hair was a protective shield that kept the world from intruding as it drifted sensually over them both.

Cupping his face as she leant forward, Anna marvelled at the strong, chiselled contours, at the sublime slopes and plains that denoted his fascinating masculine features. But it was the vulnerable, naked look of utter longing in his eyes that undid her. Stilling in shock, she hardly registered breathing.

'I thought perhaps I'd dreamt wanting you this much…but now I see that I didn't… Or if I did the dream was just a tantalising glimpse of the incredible reality that is you, Anna.'

Finding no words that could adequately describe the force of what she was feeling, Anna began to slide the buttons through the buttonholes of his fine cotton shirt with trembling fingers. When the smooth, tanned musculature underneath, with its dusting of hair, was exposed to her, she pushed the material aside, sliding her hands over the flat male nipples and taut ribcage to explore him, to feel the throb of his heartbeat beneath her palm. She was thrilled to realise that it beat with desire for *her*. Lowering her head, she pressed her lips to Dante's deliciously warm skin.

She was following the trail of silky dark blond hair towards his belly button when he made a low, husky sound, slid his hands beneath her hair and urged her eagerly upwards again. The next thing she knew he was helping remove the scrap of plain white silk that denoted her panties and sliding down his zipper.

When he placed himself at the soft moist centre of Anna's core, easing his way inside her and then plunging upwards, she threw back her head with a whimper. The very notion of pleasure broke all its bounds. It hardly seemed an adequate description for the utterly consuming sensations that effervesced through her body. Not since she'd surrendered her innocence to Dante five years ago had such violent waves of ecstatic bliss been hers. *This* was the completeness she'd longed for—the deep connection her soul had ached to experience again. The one primal force that could drive away all melancholy and doubt.

The feeling brought it unerringly home to her why she had never wanted another man since that first time with him...why she had resigned herself to being alone for ever—because no man could possibly come close to making her feel what Dante made her feel.

Utterly losing himself in their wild, urgent coupling, Dante buried himself so deep inside her dizzying heat that he swore he would melt. Expertly opening the catch on her bra, he quickly discarded the garment to fill his palms with her perfect satin-tipped breasts, stroking his thumbs across the tender nipples. Gazing up into Anna's lovely face he saw the stunning crown of burnished hair that rippled river-like down over her pale smooth skin and knew there wasn't another woman in the world to match her for beauty and grace. *Or who could crack the frozen ice round his heart.*

He should have searched for her long before this... *why hadn't he*? Unbelievable that he'd let his fear of rejection keep him from the one woman who'd selflessly given herself to him all that time ago when he was most in need.

With urgency and passion Dante's fingers bit into the soft flesh of Anna's svelte hips, holding her to him as if he could never let her go. A long soft moan followed by her ragged breathing feathered over him as she climaxed, and suddenly he couldn't hold back the tide that lapped forcefully at the shores of his own longing, and had no choice but to let it completely sweep him away...

'Come here.' He helped her lie across his chest, then wrapped his arms around her. It was a new experience for him to hold a woman like this after making love. Not just to appease her, but simply for the sheer joy of being close—to sense the beat of her heart slowly but surely aligning with his. When they finally came to live together he would enjoy that pleasure every single day he realised. Weaving his fingers through her long flowing hair Dante kissed the top of Anna's head.

She stirred, raising her face to his. 'That was rather wonderful. But now I feel absolutely incapable of doing anything else.' She smiled.

'And exactly what did you have planned for the rest

of the evening that our enjoyment of each other has interrupted, *innamorata*?'

Her smile didn't fade. Instead it grew impish, just like their daughter's. 'Well...for starters I've got a pile of ironing to do.'

'And this is essential?'

'It might not be.' Her voice lowered seductively, and renewed desire—swift and hot as a lava-flow—made Dante bite back a groan. 'It depends what distractions are on offer as an alternative.'

'You've become a shameless temptress in my absence, I see.' In one swiftly deft move Dante took hold of Anna's arms, moved her to the side of him, then captured her beneath him. The laughter in her pretty eyes instantly died. 'As long as you haven't been practising your seductive arts on some other poor defenceless male, I won't complain.'

She looked stricken for a moment. 'I swear to you I haven't.'

The tension that had suddenly gripped him at the idea of Anna being with someone else eased.

'Then is *this* the kind of distraction you were looking for, hmm?' he enquired huskily as he firmly parted her thighs and once again hungrily joined his body to hers...

'Is that an aria by Puccini you're whistling, Anna?' Pausing in his food preparation for lunch, Luigi narrowed his gaze in surprise as he studied the hotel's slim assistant manager, who had come into the kitchen to collect the menu.

'Yes, from *Madame Butterfly*. I hope you don't think I was murdering it, or being sacrilegious or something?'

'Not at all… I am only curious as to what has made you seem happy lately?'

She could have answered *a week of nights making passionate love with the Mirabelle's handsome new major shareholder*, but of course she didn't. Only Anita and her husband Grant knew the truth about her relationship with Dante. And they had agreed that the information would stay private until they returned from the month's break they were all taking while the hotel was being modernised.

The idea of her and Tia travelling to Lake Como the following day with Dante was exciting, but Anna would be lying if she didn't admit it terrified her too. Having late-night trysts with her lover was one thing, but *living together*? That was a whole other scenario entirely. And she would be totally on his turf, so to speak—dependent on his kindness and goodwill to see her through, when she was feeling unsure about the prospect of trusting a man long-term and fearing he might want to control her.

But then he *had* given her his promise that he wouldn't try and push her into anything she wasn't ready for, she remembered.

'I suppose I'm just happy at being able to take a whole

month off to spend with Tia,' she answered Luigi, poignantly realising it was an event that had not occurred since her daughter was a newborn baby. *And if it wasn't for Dante, it wouldn't be happening at all.*

Taking a couple of steps towards the chef, she clutched the paper with the menu written on it to her chest. 'A little bird told me that you're going to Provence for a French cookery course…is that true, Luigi?'

With a dismissive flourish of his hand, he sheepishly lowered his gaze. 'Signor Romano suggested it, and is paying for me to go. If we want to get a Michelin star for the Mirabelle then of course I will do it…even if French cooking is not my subject of choice. But I am surprised that a fellow Italian can be so enthusiastic about the cooking of another nation!'

'Mr Romano is well travelled and wise, Luigi. And being able to diversify the menu will help our lunchtime trade and maximise sales, so it's great that you're going to Provence.' Anna patted his arm encouragingly. 'You'll love it, I'm sure.'

'We will see.'

After a car journey to Heathrow, then a four-hour plane journey, followed by another car ride on which they took a detour for an hour to eat at a charming restaurant Dante knew, they finally arrived at his five-storey villa in Lake Como.

It was situated in prime viewing position at the lake, on a high-banked sward where the last rays of the sun played upon the surface of the water, giving it the appearance of glinting diamonds. The scent of bougainvillaea, azalea and other heady blossoms floated on the balmy Mediterranean air, rustling through Anna's unbound hair and lightly teasing Tia's wild corkscrew curls. Both females studied the house in its fairy-tale surroundings in silent awe. Having retrieved their luggage from the boot of the Mercedes that had been waiting for them at the airport, Dante stepped up beside Anna and slid his arm around her waist. As was becoming a habit, his touch electrified her.

'It's a stunningly beautiful house, Dante,' she remarked, shyly meeting his searching blue-grey glance.

'And it will be made even more beautiful by the presence of my two beautiful girls,' he asserted warmly.

It totally made her melt when he said things like that. Her heart was already his, but when he let his guard down and spoke what seemed to be his true feelings out loud Anna honestly felt as if she would follow him to the ends of the earth and back, and not care what discomfort or challenges confronted her so long as she could confront them with him.

'Is this our new house, Daddy?' Tia piped up beside them.

For answer, Dante scooped the little girl up into his arms and planted a loud, affectionate kiss at the side of her cheek. 'This is our house in Italy, *mia bambina*.' He grinned. 'But we have other homes around the world too.'

Mentally, Anna gulped. Having called her cosy basement flat in Covent Garden home for the past eight years, it was quite some dizzying leap to realise that if she and Tia were to live permanently with Dante they would be moving around quite a lot. And if the other properties he owned had anything like the stunning architecture and formidable size of this one then Anna could possibly be feeling overwhelmed for a very long time indeed!

'Let's go inside, shall we?'

'What do you think of the place now that you've had a couple of hours to acclimatise yourself?'

Dante walked up behind her as Anna stood on the balcony off the drawing room, gazing out at the stunning lake view. With a breathtaking vista of the Alps in the distance, it was guaranteed to capture all her attention. Even breathing in the warm Mediterranean air acted like a soothing salve. It made her realise how much in need of a holiday she'd been for ages.

After kissing Tia a loving goodnight, and tucking her into bed in her new bedroom, she'd been standing here ever since Dante had gone upstairs to read her a bedtime story. Now her heart leapt as he walked onto the balcony to join her. Gesturing in disbelief at the lake, with its perfectly serene surface and the twinkling lights reflected on the water from some of the surrounding buildings now that night was falling, she slowly shook her head.

'Sometimes words are inadequate, and this is one of those times. I don't think I've ever seen a more stirring or sublime scene.'

'Well, it's yours to enjoy for however long you want… you know that.'

She fell silent.

'Come inside and sit down,' he invited—but not before Anna registered what might have been uncertainty in his eyes.

Re-entering the elegant lamplit room, which was full of stunning antiques and sublime paintings, with a huge fireplace inlaid with white marble at its head, Anna smiled.

'I feel like I'm on the movie set of a film about some sophisticated Italian noble. There's so much beauty here that I can hardly take it in.'

'You are right. There *is* so much beauty.'

His low-voiced comment was loaded with meaning—meaning that Anna couldn't fail to comprehend. She couldn't glance at him without wanting him, and knew that no matter how much she tried to contain her desire he must see it in her eyes every time their gazes met.

Gesturing, she sat on the sumptuous sofa. Dante joined her. Gathering her slender palm into his, for a while he just simply turned it over and examined it—just as if it were some priceless jewel he was contemplating purchasing.

'I don't know how you can ever bear leaving this place,' she remarked, her heart quietly thudding. 'It's like paradise on earth.'

'For a long time I couldn't see it that way. But lately I've begun to see how lucky I am being able to have a home here.'

'Is this where you're from? Como, I mean?'

He let go of her hand.

'No. I bought this house because my mother loved Como and had a home here. When I was young she always fantasised about living here one day...but the truth is that she was a very simple and contented soul, and would have been happy anywhere as long as she knew I was happy.'

'She sounds wonderful.'

Dante smiled. 'She was.'

'So where were you raised, if not here?' Anna prompted him gently.

CHAPTER TEN

'I was raised in a small village inland, far away from the mountains and lakes. It wasn't anything like here.' He pushed to his feet as though the memory made him restless and uneasy. 'It didn't have the cultural delights or beautiful vistas of Como, and the people who lived there were neither rich nor privileged. But there was a strong sense of community, so I've been told. However, we didn't stay. When my father walked out on her, my mother had no choice but to move to the nearest town to try and make a living.'

'Your father walked out on you and your mother?'

'He did.' Only briefly did Dante meet Anna's gaze and hold it. 'It was a long time ago. I don't even remember him.'

'So…you don't know much about him, then?'

He grimaced. 'Only that he was British and an archaeologist. He'd been working on a dig nearby, looking for Roman ruins, when he met my mother. As far as I'm aware archaeologists aren't exactly high earners. At least I've far exceeded anything my father could have made, and my mother didn't die impoverished—as *he* left her!'

The strained silence that fell after his reluctantly voiced confession made Anna's heart sore. Dante had become a man without the love or guidance of a father, or even close male relatives, and bereft of that important bond had had to forge his own way in life. He'd had to bury what must have been a deep-seated need for love and connection from his male parent, papering it over with material pursuits and the seemingly glamorous but ultimately not permanently fulfilling rewards of success.

All Anna had yearned for as a child was the unconditional love and support of her parents. No amount of money would have made her dire situation any better. It probably would have made things *worse*, because more money would have meant her father had had more income to spend on drink. But right now it was clear to her that no matter how wealthy or successful Dante had become a big part of him still yearned for the father's love he'd never had…

Moving over to where he stood, she touched her palm to the strong heart beating beneath his fine linen shirt.

'I think you've done an amazing job of turning your life around after such a challenging start, Dante,' she told him. 'But more than what you've achieved materially, you're a good man…a man any father would be proud to call his son.'

'Am I?' For a disturbing few moments his glance was tortured. 'You only say that because you don't know what I've done to get where I am today.'

Anna's dark-eyed gaze didn't waver. 'If you've done anything wrong, in my opinion it's only that you've become too hard on yourself.'

'You're just naive—that's why you say that.'

'I had to grow up too fast—just like you, Dante—and I've learned that we don't help ourselves when we constantly criticise what we've done in the past. We did the best we knew how to do at the time. How can anyone—even *you*—do more than that?'

'You learned when you started to look for me that I had a "ruthless reputation". The papers did not lie, Anna. I did whatever I could to make my fortune. I had no scruples as long as I won the deal—as long as it meant more money and power. I was so driven I didn't even care that I helped people to lose their jobs. I certainly didn't have sleepless nights worrying about how they would support themselves or their families afterwards! Even my mother started to despair of me. She warned me against alienating good people. One day I would need trustworthy friends, she said—not phoney ones who were driven by fear and greed like I was.

'Well…it took my mother's death and then meeting you, Anna, to make me wake up to the truth of my life. To make me want to work and live with more integrity… to make me want to help people instead of exploit them for what I could get. It took me a while to change things, but when I realised that the changes I had to make had to be quite radical one of the first things I did was to revert back to my Italian name. I only used my father's name because, coming from a poor background, with only the most basic education, I wanted to distance myself from Italy and all that it meant to me. Ironic, really, when I didn't even know the man and he didn't stay around for long—'

'Oh, Dante… What an incredible journey you've had to come back to yourself.' Anna's heart was so full it was hard to keep her tears at bay.

He shook his head, as if he was uncomfortable with the tenderness in her voice, as if his painful story couldn't possibly warrant it. 'There are shadows beneath your eyes, *innamorata*.'

His hand glanced softly against her cheekbone, his blue-grey eyes as hypnotically mesmerising as the moon-lit lake outside the window, and Anna wanted to lose herself in those fascinating depths for a long time.

His next words robbed her of the chance.

'We've had a long day's travelling. You really should take the opportunity of having an early night. In the morning the housekeeper I hire to look after the villa when I'm here will arrive with her daughter, who also helps out. They'll prepare breakfast for us, and also find out if there's anything we need.'

'What are their names?'

'The housekeeper and her daughter?' Dante shrugged, as though surprised by the question. 'Giovanna is the

mother and Ester the daughter. No doubt they'll immediately fall in love with Tia when they meet her—both
of them adore children, and Ester has a little son of her
own. Anyway…like I said, you look tired. You should
have a leisurely bath, then an early night. I'll join you
later.' He turned away from her.

'I hope you don't regret sharing what you just shared
with me?' Concerned, as well as disappointed that he
seemed intent on spending the rest of the evening without her, Anna restlessly coiled a long strand of her bright
hair round her finger. 'Do you?' she pressed.

'Go to bed, Anna. We'll talk again in the morning.'

'Why don't you answer me? I don't want to go to bed
and leave you brooding here on your own.'

A faint smile appeared on his fine-cut lips as he
turned to survey her.

'So you want to be my rescuer again? Just as you
tried to rescue me from my morose mood all those years
ago?'

Fielding the comment, Anna lifted her chin. 'Is it so
wrong of me to want to reach out to you? To show you
that I care about how you're feeling?'

Remaining silent, Dante looked away again.

With frustrated tears making her eyes smart, Anna
swung round on her heel and marched out of the
room…

After watching the coloured house lights reflect off
the dark lake for a long time, Dante stepped back into

the drawing room at around one in the morning. The Campari on the rocks he'd made himself was barely touched. Leaving the crystal tumbler on a rosewood table, he stretched his arms high above his head, grimacing at the locked tension in his protesting muscles.

With everything he had in him he wanted to join Anna in the stately canopied double bed. But how could he when he knew she must secretly despise him for the way he had conducted himself in the past? It had even prevented her from getting in touch with him to tell him about Tia. No, it was Anna who was good and deserving of help…not him. Fear of failure and loss had been the dark, soul-destroying forces he'd been guided by. And because his associations with Italy had been tainted with hurt from his childhood he had fled to England to make his fortune, consciously choosing to lose his accent and forget his roots to reinvent himself as the untouchable businessman, the ice man.

All in all, it didn't make a pretty picture. Bringing Anna and Tia here had raised painful spectres from his past when he'd started to believe he had let them go. What he wanted most of all was a new start for himself and his family—not to focus on his past mistakes and feel unworthy again. But could he blame Anna if ultimately she couldn't forgive him for his deplorable history?

Intensely disliking the feeling of not having his emotions under control the way he wanted, Dante scrubbed an agitated hand round his shadowed jaw. He'd be better in the morning, he told himself. A few hours' solid sleep and he'd be more like himself again. Reaching for the button on a discreet wall panel that controlled the lighting, he pressed it, lingering for a solitary moment as the room was plunged into darkness.

Tonight he *wouldn't* seek comfort in Anna's tender arms, as he ached with every fibre of his being to do. Somehow, after practically dismissing her on her first night in Como, he didn't believe he deserved it. Instead, he would retreat to one of the other palatial bedrooms and spend the night alone…

She'd left the curtains open, and in the morning, sun streamed into the room, straight at her. Anna had to shield her eyes. Her spirits plunged in dismay when she realised that Dante hadn't joined her as he'd promised he would. He'd been absolutely right about her being tired, but she was shocked at the speed with which she'd fallen asleep. She had remained in that condition up until now too. She was in a strange country, and a strange house, as well as beginning a month's trial period of living with him. You'd think any one of those things would have kept her awake…but, no.

A deep sigh of regret escaped her. She should have stayed with him last night—should have found a way to reach him, to let him know how much she cared. If she'd stayed then he would have seen that she didn't agree with his unspoken belief that he didn't deserve love and care. He would have seen that Anna was fiercely loyal to the people she cared about. Yet she was still wary of disclosing her feelings when there was the ever-present fear that he might want to take away her autonomy…

But right now she needed to see her little girl and see how she was faring. She too had slept in a strange room, in a strange bed. Glancing at the clock by the bedside, she gasped when she saw the time. What kind of a mother was she that she could blithely oversleep and leave her child to fend for herself?

Guiltily grabbing her pastel blue cotton robe from the end of the bed, she yawned—and then couldn't resist peering out at the wrought-iron balcony and the sublime view of the sun-dappled lake. A canopied boat full of early-morning tourists floated leisurely by. She caught her breath. There was a real holiday atmosphere in the air that to Anna was just like a dream. Even more so when she thought about spending her time here with the two people she cared most about in the world…

Tia had apparently long vacated her bed. Seeing clothes scattered round the pretty room, with its lovely antique furniture and tall open windows, Anna realised she had even dressed herself. Had Dante taken her downstairs for breakfast?

Laughter and the suggestion of jovial conversation drew her to the high-ceilinged oak-beamed kitchen. As she hovered in the doorway, conscious of the flimsy robe she had hastily flung on over her white cotton nightdress, she dragged the edges together and stared. Two women—one younger, and one perhaps just past middle-age, both dark-haired, with strong-boned Italian faces and bright eyes—were bustling round the kitchen, carrying plates of food to the table and beaming at Tia, who sat there with Dante just as though she was in her absolute element.

As if he intuitively knew she was there, Dante turned in his high-backed oak chair and smiled. *Any words Anna might have been going to say utterly dried up.* Bathed in the sensual sea of his storm-coloured gaze, she felt her limbs turn as weak as cooked strands of tagliatelli.

'*Buongiorno,*' he greeted her, his low-pitched 'bed-room' voice sounding slightly husky.

Flustered, all she could manage right then was an awkward nervous smile. Rising from his chair, Dante crossed the room to kiss her cheek, his lips lingering warmly at the side of her face so that her senses were crowded by his fresh clean scent and disturbingly arous-ing body heat. His fit lean body was encased in fitted black jeans and a loose white linen shirt, and frankly he was more sinfully tempting than any honey or sugar-laden breakfast she could think of.

Unquestioningly aware of the devastating effect he had on her, he smiled for a second time into Anna's mesmerised dark gaze and curved his arm round her waist. 'Come and meet Giovanna and Ester,' he urged, leading her across the stone-flagged floor to the long oak table where the two women had paused in their serving of food to furnish Anna with twin welcoming smiles.

They greeted her in their native Italian, but then the younger woman said in faltering English, 'It is—is so nice to see you—I mean to meet you, *signorina.*'

'Please,' Anna said warmly, taking her hand, 'call me Anna.'

'Mummy? Why aren't you dressed yet?' Tia demanded, her mouth crammed with ciabatta bread and jam. 'Do you even know what the time is?'

'Yes, I know what the time is, Tia Bailey, and I know I've slept in—but I was more tired than I realised. And by the way, Miss Bossy Boots...did you forget to say good morning?'

'Sorry, Mummy, but me and Daddy have been up for ages and ages!'

'Really?'

'The early bird catches the worm...isn't that what they say?'

Seeing the teasing glint in Dante's eyes, Anna felt a rush of dizzying warmth flood into her chest. Stooping to kiss the top of Tia's curly blond head, she felt her heart warm doubly when she detected no tension whatsoever in her child about this new unfamiliar situation. Very quickly, it seemed, she had made herself quite at home.

Glancing round at the rest of the company, she became uncomfortably conscious that she was still in her nightwear. 'I'm so sorry I got up so late. I'd like to return to my room to dress, and then I'll be back down as soon as I can—if that's okay?'

'Of course it's okay.' Dante's tone was slightly irked. 'There aren't any rules about what you can and can't do here, Anna. This is your home. Giovanna will keep some food hot for you in the oven until you return.'

By the time Anna returned to the kitchen Giovanna had disappeared upstairs to make the beds, and at Dante's request Ester had taken Tia into the gardens for a while so that she could play. The woman had beamed at him, clearly jumping at the chance to spend time with his engaging little daughter.

Staring down into a mug of strong sugared black coffee—*his troubled mind hadn't allowed him to sleep at all well last night*—he glanced expectantly towards the door as Anna appeared. She was wearing a lemon tunic dress, with sleeves that ended just past her elbows and a hemline that finished just above her knees. Her long shapely legs were bare. With her stunning auburn hair left free to tumble down over her breasts unhindered she was a vision of loveliness that put Dante's already charged senses on hyper-alertness. The mere sight of her acted as an incendiary flame on his frustrated libido, making it virtual *agony* to stay sitting and not go to her and haul her urgently into his arms.

'Tia's in the garden with Ester,' he said instead, knowing that would be the first thing that would concern her. 'Is that okay?'

'Of course.' Moving to the table, Anna briefly

squeezed her eyes shut as she leaned her arms over a chair. 'I can't tell you how good that coffee smells.'

'I'll get you some.'

'It's all right. I'm quite capable of helping myself. I don't want to disturb you when you look so relaxed, just sitting there.'

She brought a mug of the steaming beverage she'd poured from the percolator back to the table, and sat down opposite him. She looked so pretty, fresh and art-less that his heart pounded with longing. Replaying their conversation of last night for the umpteenth time in his mind, he wondered if she would ever truly be able to accept him for himself and not hold his past against him.

'Tia indicated you were up early. Couldn't you sleep?'

Tumbling headlong into the liquid depths of her big brown eyes for a moment, he edged the corner of his mouth into an almost painful rueful grin. 'No, Anna… I could not sleep. Did you think I could without you in my bed?'

Blushing, she stared down into her coffee cup for long seconds. 'I would have stayed with you last night… talking downstairs, I mean.' She lifted her gaze to his. 'But you clearly didn't want me to. Whenever I try to get close to you, Dante, it seems you push me away. Do you intend on doing that for ever?'

His grin vanished. What could he tell her when his whole system was in such an agony of need? *Mental, physical, spiritual…* He could go mad with it all. He pushed his mug of coffee from him with such force that the dark liquid slopped messily over the sides. He heard Anna's shocked intake of breath even as he rose, but he was suddenly beyond worrying about anything but the powerful need to hold her, to breathe her in as though she was life-giving air in the increasing sense of claustrophobia that seized him, the prison of his past that had kept him in the dark for so long.

Hauling her out of her chair against him, Dante buried his face in her hair while his feverish hands desperately sought the warmth of her body through her thin cotton dress.

'Anna… Oh, Anna…'

Sensing her tremble, he tipped up her face and plundered her mouth until his lips ached and his heart thundered as though it would burst inside him.

'Do you want me, Dante?' As she dragged her mouth away from his, her voice sounded broken and tearful.

'Yes… Yes, I want you. I always want you! Are you going to punish me for that?'

'No, my angel.' She pushed back some of the dark blond hair that had flopped onto his brow, and her touch was so soft, so infinitely tender that Dante couldn't speak. His muscles all but screamed with the tension that built inside him, and he prayed for it to ease soon.

'You punish yourself enough without me doing the same,' she finished sadly.

Uttering a dramatic oath, he slid his arm beneath her

and lifted her high against his chest. Bereft of words, because devastating emotion had right then robbed him of the ability to speak, he carried her out through the door and up the winding staircase with its ornate wrought-iron stair-rail to their bedroom…

'What are you looking at?'

In front of the stunning cheval mirror, brushing out her long bed-tangled hair, with the balcony doors slightly ajar to allow in a delicious thermal of sultry Mediterranean air, Anna glanced over her shoulder at Dante with a smile. Bare-chested and tousle-haired, he lay back against the bank of white silk pillows with the kind of lascivious, knowing look that made her insides clench and her toes flex hard.

An impossible ache arose inside her that all but *begged* her to join him in bed for another greedy helping of wild reckless loving. She could hardly credit her own body's hungry libidinous needs. Already tingling and aching from the voracious homage her lover had paid to her in bed, Anna was seriously torn between rejoining Dante and going down to the garden to give some attention to Tia, and to thank her generous-hearted young minder for looking after her.

'I'm looking at *you*. Where else do you expect me to focus my gaze when you stand there in that thin robe that hugs every delicious curve and reminds me that I should never have let you get out of bed?'

'Well, you've got to stop looking at me like that—or

I'll be a wreck for the rest of the day because I won't be able to concentrate on anything else but you! And I want to see some of the sights of this beautiful place, Dante... For instance that medieval monastery you mentioned.'

He got out of bed, stepped into black silk boxers, then moved barefoot across the polished parquet floor to join her. Such a simple human manoeuvre shouldn't look so mouthwateringly arresting, but when a man had a body as fit and compelling as Dante Romano's, it did.

'So...a ruined medieval monastery is preferable to looking at me, is it?' he teased, his hands settling over her hips while his mouth planted a hot, sexy little kiss at the juncture of her neck and shoulder.

Anna's loosely tied cotton robe slid off one satiny shoulder as the languorous heaviness between her thighs returned.

'I—I didn't say that,' she moaned, readjusting her robe over her shoulder, then trying to disentangle herself from her lover's arms. 'What are Giovanna and Ester going to think? I already got up late, and then you persuaded me back to bed. They'll think I've got no morals or sense of decency at all!'

He laughed. It was such a spontaneous, joyous sound that Anna could hardly credit him as being the same man who had been so gripped by inner turmoil and pain earlier.

She'd cradled him in her arms for a long time after that first stormy coupling they'd fallen into when they'd come to bed, because she'd sensed he needed it. It had been all the more poignant because even a strong, powerful man like him needed the reassurance that he was cared for, she realised—even when his whole demeanour practically screamed to deny it.

'You don't have to worry about them. They are both women of the world. Besides...Giovanna put her head round the door about ten minutes after we came up here and saw that we were...busy.'

'What?' Covering her face with her hands, Anna groaned. 'Why didn't you tell me? Oh, my God...how am I ever going to look the woman in the eye again?'

'Beautiful Anna...you are making far too much of this when there really is no need. We already have a daughter. Don't you think that Giovanna and Ester have already guessed that we've been intimate?'

His teasing gaze brimmed with laughter again, and Anna lightly hit him on his toned tanned bicep. 'That's not funny!' Whirling away from him, she grabbed up her clothes from the arm of the chair, where she'd carelessly thrown them earlier, and headed for the sumptuous marble bathroom. 'You are utterly impossible—you know that?'

Dante was still grinning from ear to ear as she dramatically slammed the door shut.

CHAPTER ELEVEN

AMBLING through the quaint cobblestoned streets and alleyways of the bewitching lakeside town, Dante glanced at the titian-haired beauty beside him and wondered what he'd done to deserve the sense of satisfaction and contentment that kept washing over him.

Wearing a shift dress printed with pink poppies, her bright hair streaming loose down her back like Millais's *Ophelia*, she was the most eye-catching woman in the vicinity. More than that, the buzz he got from just holding her hand, strolling along like any other entranced tourist, couldn't be measured. All the money and success in the world couldn't match the pleasure of it. And as he walked Dante saw his home and the stunning Renaissance architecture that abounded with fresh eyes.

Another first was that for once he was simply being himself. It didn't matter who he was or where he came from. He'd shed the 'billionaire businessman' persona with alacrity, and there was such a euphoric sense of liberation about that that he almost wanted to announce it to the world. Instead, his hand lightly squeezed Anna's. In return, he received a traffic-stopping smile.

Tia was the only thing that was missing to make the day absolutely perfect. She had begged to be allowed to go with Ester and collect her son Paolo from kindergarten, after which she'd been invited to stay for lunch and to play with him for the afternoon. With Anna's consent first of all, Dante had agreed that she could go. He wouldn't have if he hadn't trusted Ester and her mother, Giovanna, completely. Giovanna had been his mother's closest and dearest friend, and that was how she and her daughter had come to take care of Dante's house for him—both when he was there and when he was away.

But although he was missing Tia already, they would all eat dinner together this evening, and he was appreciative of having some free time with Anna. This morning when they'd returned to bed she had surrendered *everything* to him. It had been as though she'd let all her carefully erected barriers down at once—even perhaps her fear of being controlled. She had simply accepted his sometimes too passionate loving with equal ardour and longing, her breathless sighs and eager exploring hands on his body letting Dante know that she was right where she wanted to be...no question.

Honestly, he had never known a woman so generous and giving—*in* bed and *out* of it. If he thought about losing her or letting her go his heart missed a beat. Frankly, it frightened him to realise how much she had come to mean to him. *Would she ever agree to marry him?* He almost felt sick at the idea she might not.

Stopping suddenly beside him, Anna pushed her huge sunglasses back onto her head to study him. 'I can hear a lot of wheels grinding and turning.' She grinned.

'What do you mean?' he asked, perplexed.

'I mean the wheels in your busy mind, Dante. What have you been thinking about?' Her brown eyes crinkled at the corners against the bright sunlight.

Pushing aside the sudden fear that arose inside him like a malevolent cloud blocking out the sun, Dante made himself smile. 'Nothing very interesting, I'm afraid. I was merely enjoying holding your hand and us being able to have this time together.'

'You weren't worrying about work? About what's going on at the Mirabelle or what million-dollar deals you're going to be making next?' Her tone was gently teasing.

'You believe all I think about is work when I'm with you?' He frowned, but then, when he might have descended into feeling guilty or frustrated that she could have such perception, he stroked his fingers across her soft cheek and followed it up with a playful pinch. 'Let me assure you, *innamorata*…my thoughts are *definitely* not about work when I'm with you. Could you doubt that after what happened this morning? There are still places on my body that throb and burn from making such uninhibited love with you. It's a wonder I can walk at all!'

Hot colour seared her cheeks and Anna lowered her gaze.

Dante chuckled softly. It was such a delight and also the biggest aphrodisiac to see her blush.

'You said there was a park that was a century old not too far away,' she commented, determinedly meeting his glance again, even though her cheeks still carried the heated evidence of her embarrassment. 'Can we go there?'

'We'll need to jump on the ferry, but why not?' he agreed, secretly delighted that he could give her such a simple pleasure.

'A ferry?' Anna beamed. 'Oh, I'd love that!'

And she did love it.

Her excitement was charmingly contagious. Dante received vicarious pleasure from travelling over the glinting blue lake on the passenger ferry with her, viewing the stunning homes that hugged the shoreline and the glimpses of medieval walls and towers in the background, even though the trip was hardly new to him and he had seen the sights many times before.

Seated on a slatted wooden bench half an hour later, in a park on the waterway that was full of Linden trees as well as a plethora of pink and red rhododendrons and white camellias, Anna swivelled round to observe Dante more closely. 'Tell me something about you that I don't know,' she urged smilingly.

Knowing there was no way of ducking out of the

question, Dante sighed, then answered quietly, 'I've been married before.'

Her beautiful smile vanished. 'Married? Not when we first met?'

'No.' His throat felt a little tight, and his voice sounded rusty. 'It was a long time before we met, Anna. I'd been divorced for about three years before I stayed at the Mirabelle that night.'

'Oh...' The relief in that breathless exhalation was tangible. 'What was her name?'

'Her name?' It never failed to astonish Dante how women always wanted to know the most inconsequential details. Another time it might amuse him. But not right now. Not when it had suddenly occurred to him that Anna might have strong reservations over marrying a man who had been divorced...especially when he told her the reason *why*. 'Her name was Marisa.'

'Was she Italian?'

'No. She came from California. I met her when I was living in New York. She worked at one of the financial establishments I dealt with there.'

'How long were you married?'

Reaching round a hand to rub the back of his neck, Dante sighed. 'Three years. She left me for someone else, if you want to know. But our marriage had hit the rocks long before that.'

'Why?'

Anna was twisting her hands together in her lap, and he sensed her definite unease. He cursed himself for bringing up the subject in the first place. To her question, 'Tell me something about you that I don't know,' he could just as easily have replied, *I'm a big fan of the opera, fine art and Italian football.* Telling her anything along the lines of the personal interests or hobbies he had would have been fine. Not that he'd ever had time for anything as normal or mundane as a hobby.

'She resented my extreme devotion to work. Whilst she loved what the rewards of that work could buy, she craved my attention too—and to be fair I wasn't as attentive of her as I could have been.'

'But it must have hurt when she left you for somebody else. Were you in love with her?'

Dante could hardly believe that he was seeing sympathy reflected in Anna's lovely dark gaze. He couldn't attest to understanding it, and was momentarily confused.

'No,' he answered honestly, 'I wasn't in love with her. Although when we first met I probably fooled myself that I was. She was vivacious, attractive and clever, and I had a couple of friends at the time who were also interested in her.' Ruefully, he shook his head. 'I suppose it was the thrill of the chase. That was the kind of thing that obsessed me then. Who could win the best deal, buy the best property, woo and win the most unattainable woman? Anyway, Marisa decided I didn't need to do much chasing after all. The wealthy lifestyle I could give her was a great incentive, you understand?'

His laugh was short and harsh. 'For a time we shared

similar aims. I was driven to succeed more and more, and so was she. She definitely wasn't the kind of woman who hankered after having a family. I suppose I kidded myself that the superficial interests we shared were enough to make our partnership work. That was until she met the young designer who came to remodel our New York apartment and had an affair with him.'

'And where is she now?'

'As far as I know she's remarried and living happily in Greenwich Village in New York, but it doesn't really concern me.' Standing up, he reached down a hand to help his silent companion to her feet. 'Let's walk on, shall we?'

Had he cared enough for his ex that he really *had* been hurt when she'd had an affair and then left him? Anna sucked in a breath, suddenly believing she knew why he seemed to have this need to take charge and control situations. Both his father and his wife had left him—it didn't matter that their marriage hadn't been a union made in heaven—and that had to have left some deep emotional scarring. It also must have pained him to learn he was married to a woman who'd seen his wealth as his greatest asset. To not be loved for yourself but instead to be wanted because of the lifestyle you could provide must be shattering.

Refusing to be downhearted because Dante had revealed he'd been married before—with his confession about his past the other night, at least now he was opening up to her a little bit—Anna smiled, sincere and relaxed. 'Yes, let's walk,' she agreed.

Walking along beside this broad-shouldered handsome man, in his sexy designer shades, with every passing female no matter what her age glancing helplessly at him, she returned her attention to the beautiful sights and scents of the park, with its plethora of flowers, ornate water fountains and sculptures. No matter what transpired between them she would never forget her month's sojourn in this magical place, nor its matchless, timeless beauty, she vowed. Even now, on only the second day into her visit, she hated the thought of leaving…

'And Paolo says I can visit him again any time I want. He speaks Italian, but his mummy told me what he said. He's so nice, Daddy. I really, really like him!'

His little daughter had scarcely paused for breath since Ester had brought her home. She'd been talking so excitedly about her visit with Ester's son that she had hardly touched the wonderful food that Giovanna had prepared for them. She'd made spaghetti Bolognaise especially because Tia had requested it.

Seated at the rectangular oak table in the woodenbeamed dining room with its huge marble fireplace, Dante had never enjoyed a meal more. Never in his life had anything felt more right than being here in Italy with Anna and his daughter.

'Well, sweetheart,' he said, beaming down into Tia's

bright eyes, 'I'm sure you will see little Paolo again very soon. But now you should try and eat something, eh?'

She took a mouthful of food, chewed it thoughtfully, then gazed back at him. 'Paolo said his daddy was dead.'

Opposite him, Anna put her fork carefully down on her plate. Dante sensed her concern. 'I know, *piccolina*,' he replied gently, laying his hand over Tia's. 'He was a friend of mine, and it was very sad when he died.'

'Does that mean that you're going to die soon, Daddy?'

Swallowing hard, Dante felt the question hit him like an iron fist in the belly. Just the thought of being separated from his child and her mother any time soon made him want to hold them in the circle of his protection with all his might—and woe betide anyone who tried to rip him away!

'Nobody knows when they are going to die, my angel… But I'm sure that heaven is not ready for me yet—especially not when I need to be here to take care of my girls!'

His throat was cramped and sore as he lifted his glance to Anna's. Just when he wanted to say more, his mobile phone rang. Glancing down at the caller ID as he took it from his shirt pocket, he saw it was from the Mirabelle.

'I'm sorry, but I really should get this. It's from Jason at the hotel,' he explained, swiftly moving away from the table and out into the corridor.

'Is everything all right?'

It wasn't the Mirabelle that was her topic of choice, Anna reflected as Dante came back into the room. What he'd said about needing to be here for her and Tia had touched her heart as nothing had ever done before, and now, setting eyes on his incredible sculpted features and winter-coloured gaze, she had an almost painfully irresistible desire to touch him and hold him. But he was holding out his phone to her, looking slightly perturbed.

'Everything at the hotel is fine… He just wanted to update me on the latest developments. Jason would like to speak with you.'

'Oh…'

Getting to her feet, and uncomfortably sensing Dante's disapproving gaze as he handed her the mobile, Anna followed his example and went out into the imposing corridor with its wall-mounted chandeliers and softly glowing lamps to take the call.

'Hi, Jason…what's up?'

'A couple of things.' His voice was friendly, but concerned. 'I heard that you were in Como with Dante. How's it going?'

'You know about me and Dante?'

'Mum and Dad told me yesterday. It was a shock, but I've had a funny feeling something's going on between the two of you ever since he showed up. Is it true that he's Tia's father?'

'Yes, it's true.'

Jason was a great colleague, and a friend, but she braced herself for his possible condemnation and hoped that if and when it came she could stay calm.

She heard him sigh. 'It must have been so hard for you, raising Tia all alone and not feeling able to contact Dante to let him know that you were pregnant. If I loved someone that much I could no more keep it to myself than fly to the moon!'

Mentally, Anna did a double-take, but her gaze was caught by the shining disc of the full moon reflecting off the dark lake outside the open casement window where the scent of heady Mediterranean blossoms floated in. Her heart squeezed with the magic of it all.

'What do you mean "if I loved someone"?'

'I can see now that you're crazy about him, that's all. You wouldn't be in Como with him if you weren't. I'm glad for you—so glad. There's nobody I know who deserves to have a happy ending more than you!'

'I *do* love him, Jason…you're right.' Acceptance and acknowledgement of her deepest feelings lapped through her like a warm velvet wave, and she crossed her arm over her waist as if to hug herself.

'So…when will the happy day be?'

'What?'

'If the man hasn't asked you to marry him then he needs his head tested.'

Chewing anxiously down on her lip, Anna glanced towards the not quite closed heavy oak door of the dining room and moved a little bit farther away from it. 'He did ask me to marry him, but I suggested we have a trial period of living together first.'

'What on earth for?'

'It makes sense, doesn't it?'

'When did loving someone ever make sense?'

To Anna's amusement, Jason sounded almost exasperated with her.

'If you love him and he loves you, and you already have the most adorable little girl together, then what's the point in having a trial period? You should be beating a path over the sun-baked cobblestones to the nearest church and sending us all invitations to the wedding quicker than I can say *la dolce vita*!'

'Should I?' she smiled. This new enthusiasm she was hearing in his voice was infectious. 'You said there were a couple of things... What else did you want to say?'

'I just wanted to let you know that included in the hotel modernisation your flat is to be converted too. I hope I haven't put my foot in it by telling you that— maybe Dante's told you about it already?'

Anna frowned. 'No, he hasn't. This is the first I've heard about it. What about all my stuff? I don't want all my belongings just thrown somewhere!'

'Don't be daft. I'll make sure everything is stored away safely—you know I will. There was just one other thing before I go.'

'Not another bombshell, I hope?'

'It's a surprise more than a bombshell. You know we were talking about romance just now...?'

The joy in his voice was hard to mistake, and Anna's curiosity grew.

'Don't keep me in suspense, Jason—tell me!'

'I think I've found my soul-mate.'

'You have? Oh, my God!' She squealed into the phone in sheer delight.

CHAPTER TWELVE

DANTE waited until Tia was in bed before confronting his fears about Anna's phone conversation with Jason Cathcart. She was sitting in front of the ornate dressing table mirror in her robe, brushing out her long fiery hair, when he walked up behind her and placed his hands on her slender shoulders. The material of the robe was thin enough for him to feel the shape of her bones, and beneath his touch he sensed her stiffen.

He wanted to say something like, *You sounded happy when you spoke to Jason,* but instead the words that came out of his mouth were sharp, bordering on accusing. 'What did Jason want? He had no business wanting to talk to you about work while you're on leave.'

Watching her expression in the dressing table mirror, he saw the satin-smooth skin between her brows pucker. 'Not even to tell me that my flat is being converted while I'm away and all my stuff is being put into storage?'

His hands reluctantly fell away as she turned to accusingly look up at him. 'I'm sorry I didn't get round to talking to you about that. With so much going on I—'

'Slipped your mind, did it? I can't pretend I'm not cross about this, Dante, because I am. That's my home that's being dismantled while I'm away.'

The subject really *had* slipped his mind since they'd arrived, and now Dante could have kicked himself. He knew how important her own place was to Anna, but there was something else he'd planned without telling her too.

It seemed now was the time to confess all.

Shaking his head slightly, he moved away across the floor. 'I owe you an apology…a big one, I know. But with the extensive refurbishment and modernisation going on at the hotel you couldn't expect your flat not to be included. However, I also want to tell you that I plan to buy a house for you and Tia—independent of whether you agree to move in with me permanently or not. A real place of your own that will come with no conditional strings attached and will be yours to do exactly what you like with.'

Without a doubt Anna was taken aback. Coiling her hair behind her ear, she didn't reply straight away, but seemed to be collecting her thoughts. When she did finally speak her expression was as touched and surprised as a small child upon whom a gift she'd never dreamt would be hers had been bestowed. 'You don't have to do that. It's an extremely generous gesture—*too* generous, really—but—'

'I want to do it for you, Anna.' Returning to stand in front of her again, Dante knew he meant it in earnest.

'I never want you to feel that your home is dependent on anyone ever again—either your employers or even *me*.'

'I don't—I don't know what to say.'

He grinned. 'Just say thank you and we'll forget about it.'

'Thank you.'

'Was the flat being converted all that Jason wanted to talk to you about?'

For some reason the question made Anna smile. 'It wasn't, actually.'

'No?' Dante sensed his irritation return. 'Then what else did he want to talk about?'

'It was a personal matter.'

'And you're his only confidante?' He was tunnelling his fingers through his hair and pacing the floor in a bid to contain his temper.

'We're good friends as well as colleagues.' Her slightly husky tone was the epitome of reason and calmness, but Dante felt his insides twist with jealousy and frustration.

'Good friends?' he said mockingly, throwing his arms wide as he came to a stop in front of her again. 'Isn't the man capable of having a male friend for a confidant?'

'Your tone suggests you think he might fancy me. Is that what's bothering you, Dante?'

'Can you blame me if it is?'

'That sounds a little possessive to me, and I don't like

it. I want to be free to talk to who I like without you being suspicious of me. I do have integrity, you know, and if I give my word that something is true then you'd better believe it.'

'If I'm concerned when you share confidences with a young, good-looking male it doesn't mean I'm trying to control or possess you. It simply means that I'm the man who has your best interests at heart, and naturally I care about who you associate with. You're the mother of my child, after all. That gives me certain rights whether you like it or not.'

Sighing, Anna fell silent for a moment, then got to her feet. 'Rights to discuss what's best for her as her father, yes,' she said. 'But those rights don't include trying to control *me*.'

'Il mio Dio!' He stared at her in disbelief. 'Did you not hear what I just said? I'm not trying to control you. Just because your father treated your mother like some—some possession he could do as he liked with, it doesn't mean that I'm cut from the same poor-quality cloth! I understand how the possibility of me being like that might scare you, Anna...' Moving closer to her, Dante slipped his hand onto her shoulder again, his heart pounding as though the starting pistol at a race had just cracked against his ear. 'I know you have great integrity, and I do believe you when you tell me that Jason is just a friend.' His lips stretched ruefully. 'But I can't help feeling a little jealous when I hear you being so animated on the phone with him.'

'Well, there's no need to be jealous.'

Her lustrous brown eyes had grown even darker, and her tone was soft, almost caressing. Now Dante's heart pounded hard for another reason. Dared he trust what he thought he saw in those silky warm depths?

Anna sighed. 'Jason told me that he's found his soulmate at last and he's in love.'

'Really?' Relief was like a dam bursting inside him.

'I was so happy for him, because he'd started to lose faith in finding the love of his life. I told him the perfect person was just waiting somewhere, and that when the time was right, they would appear. So all's well that ends well, as they say.'

'And do you believe that the perfect person is waiting for every one?'

'I do.'

'I didn't realise you were such a romantic.'

'There's a lot of things you don't realise about me, Dante!'

Now she had a maddeningly secret smile playing about her lips, and he was plunged into confusion again. If he lived to be a hundred he would never understand women...never! All she seemed to want to do was torment him.

'Is there something else you have to tell me? If there is, for pity's sake just come out and say it.' He scowled at her.

'First of all, Jason would never fancy me because

I'm the wrong sex, and secondly…I've found my own perfect person. Yes, and he's standing right here in front of me. So, Signor Romano…there wasn't the remotest need for you to be jealous.'

Looping her arms around him, she planted an achingly moist and provocative kiss against his lips. Desire was like a thunderbolt flashing through him. Catching her by the waist, Dante impelled Anna urgently against his already hardening body. Beneath the ridiculously thin robe she wore an equally insubstantial nightgown with shoestring straps. He was already visualising tearing off both garments and having her firmly beneath him.

'Marry me.' His lips, tongue and teeth clashed voraciously with hers as heat, want and devastating need broke all their bounds. Breaking off the kiss with a harsh affected breath, he cupped her face to stare deeply into her eyes. 'You *have* to marry me, Anna.'

'Of course I do… That's what I want too.'

Words failed him. All he could do right then was stare at her in wonder. Then, when he trusted he could speak, he raised his eyebrow and asked, 'When did you decide that?'

'The first time we were together, of course—when I saw you sitting in the lounge bar looking so handsome, indomitable and fierce. I knew the intimidating facade you projected wasn't the truth. Underneath I sensed you were hurting so bad you didn't know where to go or what to do. I suppose I grew up having a finely tuned antenna for people's pain. My mum's marriage was so hurtful and destroying, how could I help it?' Her eyes turned moist for a moment. 'But she believed in true love. I don't know how she held on to such a belief when she was married to a man like my father, yet she did. And she wanted the very best for me. She always told me that when I gave myself to a man it should be to the man I love. I want you to know that I do love you, Dante... I always have and always will.'

'And you forgive me?'

'For what?'

'For not trying to contact you and then changing my name, not knowing or *believing* that you might want to contact *me*, or that you would even *want* to see me again after my telling you we could only have one night together?'

'We've both made mistakes. If we can't forgive each other and move on then it's hopeless. That's not a message I want to give our daughter—that if she makes a mistake there'll be no forgiveness.'

'Ti amo.' Dante smiled, his lips visiting a series of heartfelt passionate little kisses on her eyelids, nose, cheeks and mouth. 'I love you, Anna, with all my heart and soul. Sometimes I think love is not a strong enough word to express how I feel. That evening in the hotel bar I thought I was incapable of feeling anything remotely warm towards another human being again, but you proved me wrong. Yes...' His voice grew tender. 'You reached out to me so unselfishly, even accepting

my little speech about not being able to offer you anything else but that one night. And then, like an idiot, I let you go. I've had to come to terms with some hard losses in my life, but if I lost you again… If I lost Tia now that I've discovered her…I don't think I would ever recover.'

'Well, you're not going to lose either of us, my love.'

'Is that a promise?'

With her heart in her eyes, Anna nodded. 'I swear it.'

Leaving her for just a moment, Dante crossed the room to the panel beside the door and turned down the lights. A warm scented breeze blew in off the lake.

'You can turn them off completely. There's a ravishing full moon shining just outside the window. Didn't you see it?'

Going to the balcony doors, Anna pushed them opened a little wider. For a few seconds she stepped outside to stare up at the moonlit sky. A sliver of white cloud was drifting lazily across the fiercely bright orb in the inky darkness, just as if some divine artist had painted it right there, right at that moment, for her to see. The illuminating and magical scene made her shiver with delicious anticipation.

Joining her, Dante urged her back against his warm hard chest. As Anna relaxed against him he undid the belt of her robe and slipped the garment from her shoulders. The robe was immediately cast aside onto a nearby wrought-iron chair. Then, through the paper-thin cotton of her nightdress, he cupped her breasts.

The heat from his hands, the perfect weight and shape of them against her most tender flesh, made Anna arch into his palms, her nipples puckering and hardening. Catching the rigid velvet tips between thumb and forefinger, he squeezed and tugged a little, arousing a volcanic need that poured into her centre like liquid honey heated over the hottest flame. Pressing himself against her bottom, Dante left her in no doubt he was as turned on by their arousing foreplay as she was.

Turning into his arms, Anna urgently tore at the buttons on his shirt, making him smile as in her haste her fingers fumbled and missed the openings, causing her to curse softly beneath her breath.

'What are you trying to do to me, my angel?' he mocked gently, his hollowed out cheekbones emphasised even more by that devastatingly handsome smile.

'I'm trying to get you naked! What do you think I'm trying to do?'

With one fluidly mesmerising movement, Dante ripped his hand down the centre of the fine linen material and made the buttons fly off into the unknown.

Face to face with his magnificent tanned chest, the ripple of smooth sculpted muscle over a strong defined ribcage, Anna pressed a slow, loving kiss onto the warm hard flesh matted softly with dark blond hair. Then his hands were entwined in her hair, and he lifted her head up so that he could once again claim her lips with a demanding, almost savagely passionate kiss of his own.

'When you get me naked,' he said, the timbre of his voice sounding as though it had rolled over sun-baked gravel, 'what do you intend to do with me, *innamorata*?'

Looking straight into his moonlit blue-grey eyes, Anna smiled. 'I'm going to keep you awake until the early hours of the morning…and I should tell you that I've got an extremely vivid imagination. How do you like the sound of that?'

Dante nodded. 'I like it very much, you little witch. As long as you don't fall asleep on me when I take you on the little outing I have planned for us tomorrow.'

'Oh? Where would that be?'

'I'm taking you to see my mother's house.'

'You are?'

'I want to show you what I've done with it…the new use I've put it to.'

'I'm intrigued. I would love to see where your mother lived, Dante…to get a sense of the person she was. I know she meant the world to you.'

'Well, tomorrow you will. But right now…' He fixed her with the most meltingly wicked gleam she'd ever seen. Then he scooped one strong arm under her bottom, another round her waist, and lifted her high into his arms, so that she was suddenly on even more intimate terms with his eye-catching masculine chest and his drugging male heat. 'Right now I am taking you to bed…any objections?'

Anna gulped, her heart drumming hard. 'No…I can honestly say I've no objections at all, Signor Romano.'

Brimming with anticipation, along with a genuine sense of excitement, Dante hoped that Anna and Tia would enjoy the visit he had planned to the villa on the other side of the lake.

The house he had brought them to, across the water in a luxurious motorboat, sat almost majestically back from the lakeshore, its frontage a long verdant garden that ran down to its own landing stage. He was about to reveal something about himself that he had revealed to less than a handful of friends and acquaintances, and he wanted Anna to love it. Apart from fathering his lovely daughter, it was the achievement he was most proud of.

'This was where your mother lived?' Anna commented interestedly as he helped first Tia then her out of the boat. 'It's got to be one of the prettiest villas I've seen since I've been here.'

And it *was*, Dante silently acknowledged with pride, letting his gaze travel over the ancient olive trees and tubs of glorious red, white and pink bougainvillaea dotted all around. His loving glance strayed helplessly to his bewitching wife-to-be, with her dazzling copper hair, and his lovely daughter, with her sunlit blond curls, and he knew he was the luckiest man in the world.

He pocketed the motorboat key and reached for Anna's and Tia's hands. 'Let's go and take a look inside, shall we?'

'Do you have someone looking after the place?'

'Wait and see,' he answered mysteriously, urging them cheerfully onwards.

A young woman who looked like some avant garde artist, with wild dark hair, kohl-lined eyes and row of hooped gold earrings dangling from each ear, opened the door to them with a sweet-faced baby on her hip. A burst of animated Italian issued immediately when she recognised Dante, and she flung her arms around him with obvious affection and delight.

Fielding the little stab of jealousy that pricked her, Anna strove to hold on to the ready smile she'd adopted in anticipation of meeting whoever lived in the house now. Dante made the introductions, and the young woman who went by the enchanting name of Consolata hugged Anna and Tia in turn, making much of both Anna's and her daughter's eye-catching hair. Anna's anxiety dissipated.

'Come in...yes, you must come inside,' the girl urged in enthusiastic halting English.

They stepped into the most stunning glass-roofed vestibule. It reminded Anna of one of the greenhouses for exotic and tropical plants at Kew Gardens. It was so unique and beautiful that for a few moments she didn't know what to say. *What was this place? And who was Consolata?*

Glancing at Tia, whose hand was being firmly held by her handsome father, she smiled reassuringly. But her amazingly relaxed daughter was taking everything in her stride, glancing round the glass-roofed vestibule with wonder in her big blue-grey eyes, clearly loving every second of her visit already.

A warm kiss at the side of her cheek, an intoxicating drift of musky aftershave and Dante captured Anna's hand as well. 'My mother loved this place,' he explained softly. 'See that portrait over the marble fireplace? That's a picture of her that I had commissioned when she turned sixty. She was still very beautiful.'

'I can see that,' Anna murmured, gazing up at the stunning oil painting of a woman easily as bewitching as Sophia Loren—in fact, she didn't look dissimilar.

'When I returned to Italy, almost a year after her funeral, I had it in my mind to do something in memory of her—something that she would have been proud to be a part of. I spoke with Giovanna, and she told me of the problem of some of her daughter Ester's friends who are all single mothers. She then introduced me to Consolata, and some of the other young women who are struggling to raise children on their own. I donated the house to them, so that they could all live here and raise their babies knowing they were somewhere safe and secure that wouldn't be taken away from them. Giovanna manages the place, and the children and the mothers adore her. As well as five self-contained apartments in the building, there's a communal area and two large playrooms. All the women have access to local advisory and support services. Shall we go and meet some of them?'

All Anna could do was nod dumbly. Inside, she was deluged with so much pride and joy that she could scarcely contain it. She'd always suspected that the man she loved had the biggest heart, but nothing could have prepared her for *this*. What an amazing, wonderful and generous gift! What mother wouldn't be bursting with pride at having such a son? He had honoured his mother's memory in the most touching and incredible way.

Having experienced the challenges of single parenthood, Anna guessed how much such a place like this must mean to all those mothers. It also told her how deeply Dante must have been affected by his own experience of being the son of a mother who had struggled to raise him alone. But now the man had turned his childhood adversity into something positive and inspirational for the good of others.

Curling her hand more deeply into the curve of his palm, she knew what she was feeling blazed from her eyes as she gazed back at him. Instead of fearing that marriage might mean a loss of her independence and autonomy she was now actively looking forward to joining her life with this man. And when the time came to say her vows at their wedding she would utter them with absolute conviction and love...

* * *

Leaving the yacht in the harbour, the small group of well-wishers dressed in all their finery, including a couple of professional photographers, joyfully followed the bride-to-be and her groom on foot through a small network of cobbled streets to the plain whitewashed church on the hill, with its simple wooden cross.

Halfway there Anna laughingly took off her ludicrously expensive designer shoes, because the heels kept getting stuck between the cobblestones. But she didn't mind one bit. The sun was shining and the cloudless sky was a majestic azure blue—the kind of sky you dreamed of having on your wedding day. Everything was a good omen today. She couldn't have found a bad one if she'd tried.

With the straps of her cream-coloured shoes swinging from her fingers as they mounted the stone steps to the church, Anna glanced round at her daughter. Tia was holding on to the delicate tulle train of her mother's medieval-style ivory wedding dress as though guarding it from thieves or marauders intent on snatching it away from her. The expression on her angelic little face was one of intense concentration.

They stopped for a few moments on the steps as Dante gently but firmly pulled Anna into his side. On this, their wedding day, the mere sight of her husband-to-be stalled her heart. His suit was ivory-coloured linen, and beneath it his shirt was pristine white. Pushing aside some floppily perfect sun-kissed blond hair from his brow, Anna briefly bit down on her lip, then smiled.

Today his amazing eyes weren't the colour of winter. Instead they had the hue of a calm blue lake in midsummer, and here and there the glint of dazzling diamonds shone from their depths.

'You take my breath away, Dante Romano, and it's not just because you look good enough to eat.'

He brought her hand up to his lips and kissed it, avidly observing her from beneath his lashes. 'And I am in awe of your beauty and goodness, Anna mine. Today really *is* the best day of my life…so far—because from here on in it can only get better and better.'

A couple of camera flashes went off, and Grant Cathcart—bowled over by Anna's request for him to stand as father of the bride and give her away—called out, 'Hey, you two. The kissing's meant to happen *after* the wedding…not before it!'

'Yes, Mummy and Daddy—didn't you even know *that*?' Hand on hip, Tia let go of the train of Anna's dress for a moment and affected exasperation. As her parents and guests laughed, her look of exasperation was quickly replaced by one of horror as she saw the ivory train trailing over the stone steps. She grabbed it up again. 'I hope this hasn't got dirty—because if it has then I shall be *very* cross with both of you!' she declared.

'How on earth did we produce such a bossy child?' Dante laughed.

'It's got to come from *your* side.' Anna grinned. '*I*

was the personification of sweetness and light, growing up.'

His eyes narrowing, Dante tipped his head to the side, pretending to be doubtful. 'You sure about that, *innamorata*? Only I definitely recall one or two memorable occasions when the ability to be bossy seemed to come very naturally to you.'

'I'll make sure you pay for that remark later,' she whispered, her mouth trembling with humour as Dante once again pulled her towards him.

Hefting a noisy sigh, Tia turned round to the guests gathered at the base of the steps, in her ivory-coloured bridesmaid dress and pretty crown of delicate flowers, and threw up her hands. 'Everybody hurry up and go inside the church—before they kiss *again*!'

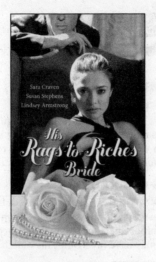

THE RELUCTANT DUKE
by Carole Mortimer

Forced to return to his family's seat, Lucan St Claire takes beautiful PA Lexie Hamilton with him. Lucan, however, has no idea that his new assistant isn't quite what she seems…

THE DEVIL WEARS KOLOVSKY
by Carol Marinelli

Swearing revenge on the Kolovskys, who abandoned him, Zakahr Belenki determines to destroy their fashion empire! Then he meets his secretary, Lavinia. Her honesty and passion for her job make Zakahr's conscience waver—and inflame his desire…

PRINCESS FROM THE PAST
by Caitlin Crews

Marriage to Prince Leo Di Marco was no fairytale, so Bethany Vassal ran away, hoping the man she loved would come and find her. Now the time has come for Leo to produce a royal heir—and Bethany must return to the castle whence she fled!

INTERVIEW WITH A PLAYBOY
by Kathryn Ross

Marco Lombardi *hates* journalists. Whisking reporter Isobel Keyes away in luxury seems like damage limitation—until she sparks his interest. Now Marco *wants* to kiss and tell…

On sale from 4th February 2011
Don't miss out!

Available at WHSmith, Tesco, ASDA, Eason and all good bookshops

www.millsandboon.co.uk

Live life to the full - give in to temptation

Four new sparkling and sassy romances every month!

Be the first to read this fabulous
new series from 1st December 2010
at **millsandboon.co.uk**
In shops from 1st January 2011

Tell us what you think!
Facebook.com/romancehq
Twitter.com/millsandboonuk

Don't miss out!

*Available at WHSmith, Tesco, ASDA, Eason
and all good bookshops*

www.millsandboon.co.uk

&◆RIVA™

Walk on the Wild Side
by Natalie Anderson

Jack Greene has Kelsi throwing caution to the wind—it's hard to stay grounded with a man who turns your world upside down! Until they crash with a bump—of the baby kind…

Do Not Disturb
by Anna Cleary

A preacher's daughter, Miranda was led deliciously astray by wild Joe… Now the tables have turned—he's her CEO! But Joe's polished exterior doesn't disguise his devilish side…

Three Weddings and a Baby
by Fiona Harper

Jennie's groom vanished on their wedding night. When he returns, he has his *toddler* in tow! Jennie can't resist Alex's appeal and, for a successful businesswoman, one kid should be easy…right?

The Last Summer of Being Single
by Nina Harrington

Sebastien Castellano, prodigal city playboy, has mysteriously returned home to his sleepy French village. Now he's reminding single mum Ella how much fun the *single* part can be!

On sale from 4th February 2011
Don't miss out!

Available at WHSmith, Tesco, ASDA, Eason and all good bookshops

www.millsandboon.co.uk

MILLS &
BOON®

are proud to present our...

Book of the Month

Prince Voronov's Virgin
by Lynn Raye Harris

from Mills & Boon® Modern™

Paige Barnes is rescued from the dark streets of
Moscow by Prince Alexei Voronov—her boss's
deadliest rival.   Now he has Paige unexpectedly in
his sights, Alexei will play emotional Russian
roulette to keep her close...

Available 17th December

Something to say about our Book of the Month?
Tell us what you think!

millsandboon.co.uk/community
facebook.com/romancehq
twitter.com/millsandboonuk

2 FREE BOOKS
AND A SURPRISE GIFT

We would like to take this opportunity to thank you for reading this Mills & Boon® book by offering you the chance to take TWO more specially selected books from the Modern™ series absolutely FREE! We're also making this offer to introduce you to the benefits of the Mills & Boon® Book Club™—

- **FREE home delivery**
- **FREE gifts and competitions**
- **FREE monthly Newsletter**
- **Exclusive Mills & Boon Book Club offers**
- **Books available before they're in the shops**

Accepting these FREE books and gift places you under no obligation to buy, you may cancel at any time, even after receiving your free books. Simply complete your details below and return the entire page to the address below. You don't even need a stamp!

YES Please send me 2 free Modern books and a surprise gift. I understand that unless you hear from me, I will receive 4 superb new books every month for just £3.30 each, postage and packing free. I am under no obligation to purchase any books and may cancel my subscription at any time. The free books and gift will be mine to keep in any case.

Ms/Mrs/Miss/Mr _____ Initials _____

Surname _____

Address _____

_____ Postcode _____

E-mail _____

Send this whole page to: Mills & Boon Book Club, Free Book Offer, FREEPOST NAT 10298, Richmond, TW9 1BR